Exile

Peg Tittle

Rock's Mills Press
Oakville, Ontario
2019

The author would like to acknowledge funding support for this project from the Ontario Arts Council, an agency of the Government of Ontario.

For information, including Library and Archives Canada Cataloguing in Publication data, please contact Rock's Mills Press at:
customer.service@rocksmillspress.com.

ISBN-13: 978-1-77244-161-1 (paperback)
ISBN-13: 978-1-77244-162-8 (ebook)

www.rocksmillspress.com

Exile

1

LJ hurdled over the turnstile, clearing it easily, and ran laughing after K and Dub. The subway was crowded, and the three of them made little effort to avoid knocking into people. In fact, they went out of their way to do just that. If the people they hit fell over, all the better. K grabbed someone's knapsack, Dub snagged someone's bag of groceries, and LJ snatched someone's laptop. They ignored the shouts of protest, revelled in them actually, and squeezed through the closing doors of one of the cars just as the train started to move.

The three of them claimed half a dozen empty seats. A man in his thirties tensed a little and moved closer to his nine-year-old son. He carefully faced forward, minding his own business.

K rummaged through the knapsack he'd grabbed. Nothing but books in it, which he tossed aside in disgust.

"What you got?" he said to Dub and LJ.

Dub upended the bag of groceries. Apples, oranges, an onion, and several peppers rolled onto the seat and then off, onto the floor.

"Nothin', man!"

LJ had opened the laptop, turned it on, and seemed to be pressing keys at random.

"Bunch of files … I dunno … Don't see nothin'," LJ muttered to himself.

"Delete 'em," K said. Then laughed.

The man looked over quickly with alarm, a reflex. K stared him down. The man said nothing, and pointedly resumed minding his own business.

K moved to sit closer to the man. "Goin' to the game?"

he asked. He used a fake-nice voice, but everything K said sounded like a challenge. Because it was.

"Yes, my son and I, we have tickets," the man replied, pleasantly enough though he was clearly nervous.

"Oh, yeah? Can I see 'em?"

The man pulled out two tickets and naïvely handed them to K, who promptly pocketed them.

"Thanks, man!" K snickered and moved back to Dub and LJ.

The man blanched with anger. And humiliation. But he said nothing. Did nothing.

"Dad!"

"Shh."

"But he—"

"Doesn't matter," he looked at his son, pleading, begging him to understand the warning in his eyes. The boy closed his mouth, then looked straight ahead, following his dad's lead. The man put his arm around his son's shoulders and squeezed.

The train stopped. The man and his son got off, quickly. LJ pressed the 'Delete' button, tossed the laptop aside, then joined K and Dub, who had also gotten off.

"Later, men," K said to Dub and LJ, then sauntered off. Dub looked around a little, lost and helpless, then tagged along behind K. LJ turned and headed up the stairs, out into the streets.

Five minutes later, LJ passed a high school. The track team was having a practice. He paused and watched through the chain link fence, a bit wistful, a bit angry.

As he continued to walk along the broken sidewalk, passing an odd mix of scrappy houses and run-down apartment buildings, Mr. Morgan and Mr. Rodriguez continued to work the street, walking behind a slow-moving garbage truck, picking up the garbage cans and emptying them into the truck. Mr. Morgan stared intently at LJ. LJ happened to glance in Mr. Morgan's direction, but looked right through him.

2

The courtroom looked a little like one of the rooms for rent at the local Legion or Rotary Club, but was, in fact, one of about ten such rooms in the city courthouse. All the pomp and circumstance was expensive and had been dispensed with long ago. It was unnecessary.

There were very few people in the room. Judge Wellington was seated behind a large table at the far end, across from the main entrance. Her assistant, the JA, sat beside her. They each had a laptop on front of them containing the docket and the relevant files. The proceedings were recorded by the room system. Two guards stood at the main entrance, and another pair stood at a side entrance which connected to a hallway leading to an outside door. Just outside that door, a van was parked, its door open and connected to the building with one of those portable accordion tunnels one sees at airports.

Benches filled the main space. On the Judge's left, several men sat in them as if they were bleachers. Rather than pews. On the right, the benches contained small clusters of people, women and children mostly, family and friends of those waiting to appear before the Judge. Family and friends at a picnic or a park outing gone horribly wrong.

"Andrew William Smith?" the JA called out.

A heavy young man in a crew cut rose and approached the table. He stood before the Judge, his folded hands hanging loosely over his crotch. It was a common posture among a certain kind of man. When he found himself standing in front of a woman.

"Are you Andrew William Kessel?" the Judge asked.

"Yes, ma'am."

"How do you plead," she glanced at her screen, "to the counts of battery and aggravated assault occurring during the evening of Monday, April 20, 2027 at 17 Young Street?"

"Guilty."

"This is your first offence, is that correct?" She glanced again at his file.

"Yes, ma'am."

"What were you thinking?" She looked straight at him.

"Excuse me?"

"What were you thinking? Why did you assault—" she checked the record before her, "James Everett?"

"He pushed me."

"But you beat him so badly, he is now in the hospital."

"Yes." He didn't seem ashamed. It was as if that fact had nothing to do with him.

She turned back to the file, and the court waited while she read the detailed description of the battery and assault.

"You had a knife?" Why was she surprised?

He nodded, a single, quick nod, then remembered that he had to speak for the record. "Yes, ma'am."

She turned from his file, then sighed. "Do you know what a colostomy bag is?" she asked him.

"No, ma'am."

She sighed again. "I'd like you to meet with James, and I want you to listen to what he has to say to you. You will spend three hours, handcuffed, in his presence. You can just stare at each other for the three hours, but I hope you will talk."

He nodded again.

"Then I'd like—have you heard of the four-step program?"

"No, ma'am. I've heard of the twelve-step program."

"Yes, well," she said, with a slight grimace, "we don't believe in a higher power here. The first step is knowledge. You are to spend one month—these are court orders—one month in an ER learning human anatomy and physiology, specifically what happens to various parts of the body when they are subjected to fists, baseball bats, knives, and bullets.

"Then you are to take a course that will develop your imagination. So even when you don't see the blood, and torn organs, and shattered bones, you will be able to imagine said blood, and torn organs, and shattered bones."

Another quick nod.

"Step three is control. You are to work with a therapist to develop self-control. If you can stop yourself long enough to foresee, to imagine, what will happen as a result of what you do, perhaps you'll choose more wisely what to do and what not to do.

"Lastly, the court orders you to take a course in conflict resolution, so the next time someone pushes you, you might say 'Excuse me, sir, but I believe I was here first'—"

The man started to protest, but she cut him off.

"—or, better yet, just walk away." She looked at him, challenging him to come right out and say—something. He was silent. Hopefully mute with the struggle to imagine—just walking away.

"Dismissed." She banged her gavel—they had kept that accessory—and one of the guards led Andrew William Kessel from the court.

The JA made an entry into the record, closed the file, and opened the next.

"Leroy James Wagner?" he called out.

LJ got up, then shuffled forward to slouch before Judge Wellington.

"Are you Leroy James Wagner?" she asked.

"Yeah. Yes."

"How do you plead," she opened the file, "to the counts of illegal entry, property damage, theft, and assault, occurring during the afternoon of Tuesday, April 21, 2027 at the South and Main subway station?

"Guilty, I guess."

She looked up at him.

"Guilty," he amended.

"As this is your third conviction, you are hereby exiled."

As the JA made an entry into the record, the Judge motioned to one of the guards, who led LJ out the side door.

An hour later, Judge Wellington sat at a table in the lunchroom having her lunch. Half a tuna sandwich and a nectarine. Judge Rose joined her, holding his tray in one hand, laden with French fries, a burger, and a salad, and a newsletter in the other.

"Have you seen the stats? Down 300!"

"Nation-wide?" she asked, quickly wiping her hands on a napkin, then taking the newsletter he held out to her.

He nodded, settling into the chair opposite.

"New intakes? Per week?" She found it hard to believe and was impressed. She scanned the rest of the front-page article, a report on the success of the new three-strike law. It had been put into effect a year ago, after extensive debate, during which much mention was made of Australia's history and the relatively harsh Canadian winters. A surprisingly high number of people supported the new law, the model of inalienable human rights apparently having given way to one in which all rights had to be earned and could be forfeited.

Once a person was sixteen. That had been one of the many issues of debate. Many people thought the age of personal responsibility should have been set at eighteen, but, when they were presented with the crime statistics for men between sixteen and eighteen, quickly changed their minds. As early as 2008, research had revealed that over 30% of all men had been arrested for something or other by the time they'd turned eighteen. It was like there was something fundamentally wrong with men. Perhaps the Y chromosome had mutated so much, the males were no longer homo sapiens. Add testosterone and little or no compensatory upbringing—'Listen, next year or the year after, something's gonna hit you like, not like a ton of bricks, more like a forced overdose of an incredibly strong constant-release character-changing drug, and you have to be ready to resist, it'll take everything you have—' Whoever said civilization was in greatest danger from its fourteen-to-twenty-four-year-old males was right.

True, many men had made huge contributions, to society, to civilization. But no doubt women could have too, given the same sorts of chances. Maybe, with so many men out of the way, that would happen ...

"Still thinking of resigning?" Judge Rose asked, taking a forkful of the salad. He'd made a deal with himself that he couldn't start on the fries and burger until he'd finished the salad.

"I am," Judge Wellington replied.

He chewed, thinking of arguments that could change her mind.

"How's your docket?" he asked.

"My docket's fine," she smiled. "I'm getting a full forty-five for lunch."

He raised a forkful of salad in salute.

"And the wheels of justice are turning faster, I'll grant you that. No one spends two years in prison anymore just waiting for their day in court."

"But then—"

"And there aren't any more frequent flyers. I'm not convinced it's working as a deterrent, but if they're not here, they can't—"

"So …" he looked at her questioningly.

"It's too simple," she said.

"Occam's Razor," he returned.

"He was referring to explanations, not solutions," she said. "Even so, this is not what he meant by 'simple' and you know it."

"True enough," he conceded, taking the first bite of his burger. And suppressing a moan.

"Three thefts-under will never equal three rapes," she stood up and began to pack away her reusable lunch things, "Of your ten-year-old daughter."

He chewed as quickly as he could, swallowed, then belatedly called out after her. "It just needs to be tweaked a bit."

That was certainly true, she thought as she left the lunchroom. And possible. Even likely as time went by. But in the meantime …

What about wrongful conviction? It happened. Maybe not three times to the same person, but if it happened just once, out of three times, the person would be exiled for two, not three, strikes. And though she hated to admit it, race and class had to do with that likelihood.

And where was motive? That was another one of her concerns. What about all those people who, in one way or another, had no choice but to do the things they did?

Over two thousand years, and they had yet to figure out what to do with bullies. Despite the innocuous label, they remained perhaps their greatest problem. On every street. In every neighbourhood. In every country. Men bullied others to do their dirty work, with threats they would be all too happy to follow up on. Sell these drugs, beat up this person, forge these documents, get your testimony wrong—or you'll have an accident. Or maybe your kid will disappear one day on the way home from school.

Exile was a perfect solution, she thought, but at the moment it cast too wide a net.

3

LJ was slumped in a chair across from a uniformed woman who was quickly tapping on her keyboard. They were in a plain, functional office. LJ looked at the nameplate on the desk, which was no more informative than the sign on the door.

"So you're an 'Escort Officer'"? he asked, mockery mixed with mild curiosity.

"That's correct," she said as she pressed 'Enter', then opened the next file, which was LJ's, and quickly scanned its contents.

"What's that, the new word for 'Parole Officer'?" he asked.

She looked at him then, first dully, then with some disbelief.

"You don't know?"

"Don't know what?" he asked, a little belligerently.

"This is your third offence, is that correct?" She looked again at her screen.

"Yeah, so?"

"Do you have somewhere to go?"

"What do you mean?"

"Have you found a society that will accept you?" she rephrased her question.

LJ laughed. "What, I have to find my own prison?"

"You're not going to prison," she said flatly. "This is your third time."

"Yeah …" What was her problem?

"You really don't know, do you?" She stared out the window.

"Don't know what?" LJ asked again, annoyed.

"You haven't a clue as to the consequences of your actions," she murmured, then turned back to face LJ. "Well, that's just one more reason."

She could see his anger, his incomprehension, simmering on his face.

"Look," she explained then, "the first time you break our laws, the laws of this society, we try to rehabilitate you. Make you understand, and, hopefully, change."

"Yeah, that was a joke."

"Obviously," she said dryly. "Second time, you get punishment. You were sent to prison," she looked again at LJ's file, "for two years. And yet here you are again."

He opened his mouth, but she didn't give him a chance.

"Third time, well, given your inability or unwillingness to follow the rules of this society, you should live in some other society, yeah? If you have found a society willing to take you, we will provide escort. If not, we will escort you into exile."

"What do you mean?"

"We're kicking you out."

4

"No pack?" the escort guard asked LJ the next morning as he was brought toward the waiting van. "You're allowed."

"What?" He had no idea what she was yammering on about. Yesterday, that woman, the 'escort officer,' had gone on and on about how he was allowed twenty-four hours and access to CTs. Communication technologies. He didn't care. She could talk at him all she wanted, he didn't care.

"Never mind," the guard said then. The answer to her question was obvious.

"Just the one?" she asked her partner as he secured their transport then closed the door.

"Yup."

Hm. At this rate, she thought, she might soon be out of a job.

Her partner pulled the van out of the lot and into traffic. They were quiet as they moved through the city, following the route provided by the onboard computer. They didn't know until they were on the road which route they'd be given. Or to which door they'd be directed. It reduced hijacks.

LJ watched the city pass by. Good riddance, he thought.

After about twenty minutes, they were on the expressway heading out of the city. Ten minutes after that, they were in the countryside.

LJ leaned forward to look. He'd never been. In the countryside.

"So, have you been an escort guard long?" she asked her partner, settling in. It was going to be a long drive.

"Yeah, I guess," he kept his eyes on the road. "I transferred from MaxSec shortly after the ThreeStrike."

"Really? What was it like? I mean, do you think the ThreeStrike is better? I read that it's unfair because—"

"Don't believe everything you read. Yeah, all crimes count the same. And yeah, maybe that's not fair. But from my point of view, ThreeStrike is better. Way better."

"What makes you say that?"

"MaxSec is—was—inhumane. What it does to the prisoners. What it does to the guards."

She waited for him to continue.

"Imagine what it would be like to be locked up in a small cage—essentially, they are," he insisted, noticing her slight protest, "even though they can move around some. They get to do that only a few times a day, and every step they take is policed."

He glanced in the rear view mirror to check on his transport.

"So imagine what it would be like to be locked up in a small cage—and know it's for the rest of your life."

The navigational system indicated a turn ahead. He looked in the side mirror before making a lane change. Guess they were taking the scenic route, he thought.

"Have you ever seen those movies," he continued, "about what it would be like if it were the last day on earth? Some people just end it early, because they've got nothing to live for anymore, they've got no future. And the rest of them just go out and party hard, hard as they can, wrecking stuff …

"That's what it's like for people who are in MaxSec for life. Suddenly they've got no future.

"And yet, they are alive the next day. And the day after that. And the day after that. They've got years ahead of them, but they can't have any plans, any goals. They've got no hopes, no dreams. There's no point."

She was starting to see the problem.

"So they go crazy. Literally."

He stared ahead at the mostly empty highway.

"And the ones that were crazy to begin with get worse."

"Didn't the ones with mental illness get treatment?"

"No."

She waited for him to continue.

"I've seen men—eat themselves."

She glanced over, a grin— He was absolutely serious.

"The ones who were mentally ill weren't supposed to be there in the first place, I guess, but maybe there wasn't room for them in the hospitals. There certainly weren't enough psychiatrists to go around. Guys had to wait months for a half-hour session.

"And in any case, as I say, a lot of them became crazy after they arrived. No one could stay sane in a place, in a situation, like that."

He paused, remembering. Again, she waited.

"Especially if they get Solitary. If you're in Solitary, you get one hour of fresh air every day. You get one shower every two days. The rest of the time, twenty-three hours of twenty-four, you're in a concrete room barely bigger than the average bathroom. One guy was in Solitary for two years. When he came out, he—he wasn't even human.

"Eventually almost all of them want to kill themselves," he continued. "Except for the ones having too much fun trying to kill everyone else.

"And I mean that literally. They'd kill each other, or try to, over nothing. And then laugh as the other guy lay dying.

"It was a way to break the monotony. Entertainment. Sure, they could watch TV—"

"And be entertained by more killing," she said wryly.

He looked over and nodded.

"It was probably also a way to do something, to have

some control, some power, to make some difference, in their lives.

"You understand these are people who— It's not like they could amuse themselves inside their heads or make a difference by solving the mysteries of the universe."

They watched the bleak landscape go by.

"No wonder so many wanted to just end it all," she said.

"But they couldn't," he said angrily. "That was part of the problem. We weren't allowed to let them to. They'd beg— And that's just—"

"But suicide is legal," she looked over, surprised and confused.

"I know! That's what's so sick about it. But our job was to 'protect' them. So we were supposed to stop them if they tried. We were supposed to make sure they didn't have access to anything that they could use."

"So you'd have hundreds of—"

"Thousands—" he corrected. "They'd pace. Back and forth, back and forth, just like animals in a zoo."

"No wonder you transferred."

He nodded grimly.

"It got so bad—some guys don't take the job home with them, but how can you not take that shit home with you?" He looked over at her, as if genuinely wanting to know.

He continued. "You come to always expect the worst. In people. In life."

"That would be a rational response. You always see the worst."

Again, he nodded.

"And you yourself—you start becoming just like them. There was a young guy once, the boiler was acting up, there was cold air blowing into his cell, and he kept asking for an extra blanket, but none of the guards would give him one. The kid was so fucking cold he couldn't sleep. This had gone on for three days before I got on shift. And then they all started calling me a fucking Elizabeth Fry for giving the kid an extra blanket. And I thought, what the hell is wrong with people?

"I mean, sure, the kid deserved to be in prison, they all do, no question. The shit they've done, most of them have no respect whatsoever, but—"

"Are you familiar with Zimbardo's prison experiment?" she asked. "The one done back in 1971?"

He nodded. It was a standard in Psych 101.

"But it's not just the cruelty," he said. "It's also the … vigilance. You start watching your back, all the time, because you're always expecting—

"Because you're locked up too. The only difference is it's for ten hours a day, not twenty-four," he grimaced.

He stopped to listen to the navigational system again and turned at the next sideroad.

"So, at least with the ThreeStrike," he nodded to the back of the van, "if LJ here ever decides he's had enough, he can do something about it. He still has his dignity, his autonomy."

A couple hours later, they stopped to trade places. They had passed the occasional town, several very long stretches of forest, and one or two rivers. They'd even seen a few lakes in the distance. It was pretty country.

An hour after that, following the navigational system's directions, the escort guard slowed and drove onto the shoulder of a long stretch of highway. There was nothing but scrub on either side. She turned off the ignition and put the vehicle in park.

LJ woke up. He had no idea where he had been taken, but he wasn't too concerned. About anything. Which was, of course, his problem.

In fact, he'd simply been taken north. When the States had annexed Canada, they'd designated chunks of northern Quebec, Ontario, Manitoba, and Saskatchewan as exile. "The First Nations'll stop 'em," everyone said. Forgetting how successful that had been back in 1492.

The guard got out and stood by the back door. As soon as her partner joined her, they opened the door and helped LJ manage his cuffs to exit the vehicle. He stretched, then stared at the bleak landscape. Then he noticed a car parked in the distance. For a second, he thought it might be K and Dub, but it looked like Mr. Morgan who was standing beside it. Which didn't make any sense.

"This way," the guard said, looking at the electronic device she held in her hand and leading her partner, who had a firm grip on LJ, to a spot about thirty feet off the road. She swung the device to the right and then to the left, confirming her position.

LJ looked around him, then noticed that something wasn't quite right with the view. A long stretch to the left and to the right of where they were looked fuzzy.

"There's an invisible wall surrounding exile," the guard explained, when she noticed the puzzlement on his face. "It sort of reflects the view."

LJ nodded, not really understanding. Or caring.

"This is the door," she said, as she deactivated that portion of the wall. Her partner walked LJ toward it.

"Escort officer said this wasn't a prison," LJ said then. Starting to put two and two together.

"Oh the wall isn't here to keep you in," the guard handling him said. "It's here to keep you out. We don't want you."

LJ looked at him, inexplicably a little hurt.

"Hey, only because you so clearly don't want us," he said. "Right?"

LJ ignored the question.

"So what do I do in there?" he asked.

"Whatever you like," the first guard answered, as her partner took off LJ's cuffs and nudged him forward. "Isn't that what you want?"

5

LJ walked through and the world behind him disappeared.

He saw that a rough path led away from the wall, so he followed it. Nothing else to do.

Five minutes. Ten minutes. Fifteen minutes. After twenty minutes of walking without seeing anyone, anyone at all, he was starting to feel a bit weird. He would not admit to fear, of being alone, but he was definitely relieved to see, after twenty-five minutes, three people in the distance approaching him.

When they got close enough, they beat him up and stole his shoes.

It happened so fast, he didn't have a chance. That's what he told himself. On his hands and knees, trying to catch his breath from a hard punch. He eventually got to his feet, bruised, battered, and bleeding from a cut lip, but nothing seemed broken, so he was able to carry on. Far more slowly. Especially now that he was barefoot. Good thing it wasn't winter.

When he next saw someone, about an hour later, he made a painful dash for a nearby boulder and crouched behind it. A moment later, he twisted to peek around the edge, stifling a groan, and saw that the other person had run away.

He relaxed a bit, and leaned back against the rock. He was hot. He was tired. He was thirsty. He was hurt. He was hungry.

Maybe he'd just stay here a while, he thought. Maybe

he'd just stay here for the night. He could grab some sleep and start fresh in the morning.

It was then that he saw the snake making its way from the top of the boulder where it had been sunning. LJ jerked away, stumbling.

He decided to continue on the path. He had no idea where it was going, but it must go somewhere, right? Maybe it went to a river or something. He could really use a river. Or something.

Six difficult hours later, he found that the path did indeed go to a river. Intensely relieved, he gingerly bent down to take a long drink. Then he carefully arranged himself on the bank to soak his feet. The cool water felt very, very good. And it washed away the dirt and blood from his scraped feet. He took his t-shirt off, rinsed it, then put it back on. That felt good too.

"Just got here?"

LJ wrenched around and scrambled to his feet, wincing as he did so and nearly falling. He found himself facing a balding, middle-aged guy, standing in a tattered shirt and a worn pair of shorts. He looked like an insurance agent on a Caribbean vacation. A half-star Caribbean vacation.

"This morning," LJ told him.

"And you got this far before dark?" The man sounded impressed. "And with no shoes even."

LJ looked at the man's feet then, and saw that he wore sandals. Not leather sandals. Pathetic, falling apart, sandals made out of—weeds?

"They hang out near the border," the man said. "Waiting for guys like you."

"Guys like me." What was that supposed to mean?

"New guys. Guys not expecting it."

"Why don't you do something about it then?" LJ asked, peeved.

"Me? Now why should I do something about it?" The man looked at LJ as if he really wanted to hear his answer.

"Well, you live here, don't you?"

"Your point?"

LJ didn't know what his point was or on some level realized he was the last one to spout off about law and order or civic duty. So he said nothing.

"I'm John," the man said then, reaching out his hand.

"LJ." He eased himself back down, then thought to ask, before John left, "Hey man, can I sleep here? Is it safe?"

"Yeah," John replied, settling himself nearby against a tree. "I'll watch your back."

LJ wasn't convinced it wasn't a con, but he was too exhausted to worry about it—he fell asleep almost instantly.

About an hour later, two men approached John, quietly so as not to wake LJ.

"Well?" Ed, the tall, pony-tailed, First Nations man asked. Anthony, the handsome black man with him, looked carefully, but quickly, at LJ, as if scanning a musical score to get the gist of the piece.

"Maybe," John replied.

Ed nodded, satisfied, as did Anthony, and the two of them left.

Mid-morning, LJ woke. He got up, feeling worse than when he'd fallen asleep. He walked carefully to the river and took another drink.

"You're awake," John had been watching him from his spot against the tree.

Startled, LJ turned too quickly and let out a groan.

"Good," John said. "I'll take you over to the beach to meet the others. You can go for a swim there, if you like."

"Okay," LJ said. The swim would be good. And maybe they had food. He was hungry.

It took almost half an hour to reach the end of the river. They skirted a weedy, mucky section where it fed into the lake, then just around a treed point, they arrived at the edge of a small beach. LJ sighed as his feet sunk into the sand.

"Any women here?" he asked John, as they headed toward the half dozen people in the distance.

John gave him a look. Unimpressed.

"Thought maybe one of 'em could make me a pair of shoes," LJ explained.

John gave him another look. Even more unimpressed.

"I know of only two," he said. "One got raped to death. The other died giving birth."

LJ glanced at John. Was he serious?

They continued walking toward the beach.

"So what are you in for?" LJ asked.

"You mean why was I exiled? Income tax evasion."

"That's it? No assault or nothin'?"

"Nope. And you?"

"Petty theft. Sort of."

They kept walking.

"Income tax evasion," LJ said, having thought about it. "You must be smart."

"Nope," John said. "I'm about as stupid as you. Thinking I could or should get something for nothing. Be different if I'd withheld only the portion that paid for weapons, or that subsidized churches, but no, I withheld it all," he sighed. "Even the money that paid for roads, schools, and hospitals. I was pissed off at the government. Don't know what I was thinking."

"Probably weren't thinking," LJ said. "Just like me."

John looked over, surprised.

"But roads and schools," LJ said, "they're free, so—"

"Nothin's free, 'cept maybe the air. 'Free' just means someone else paid for it. That's what income tax is all about."

When he looked over at LJ and saw the blank look on his face, he realized he'd never paid income tax. "You've never held a job?!"

LJ shrugged. He'd never needed one. His mom had put food on the table, she'd paid the rent, he'd never really thought about it.

"So what do people do for shoes around here?" His most pressing concern. Besides, increasingly, hunger.

"Well, I've made my own." John stopped to lift his foot and show LJ his handiwork. "It's a lot of work and they don't last very long, but—" he recalled LJ's earlier comment, "that's women's work. Right. Well, there's the dump."

"The dump?" What would a dump be doing here?

"Yeah, people must've lived here before it was turned into exile, and outaways," he gestured vaguely, "there's what must have been a dump. It's pretty much picked over by now, but—" he stopped, seeing the disgust on LJ's face, "that's beneath you. Right."

A rabbit suddenly appeared at the edge of the bush, no doubt heading for a drink of water, but when it saw them, it turned quickly and disappeared back into the bush.

"Hey, I could catch a rabbit," LJ said. "Make me a pair of rabbitskin shoes."

"Yeah … Could you catch a rabbit?" John was interested. "Really?"

"Maybe. If I had shoes."

John smiled. "If you had shoes, you could get shoes."

A moment later, he added, "Apparently someone tried that once. Didn't prepare the skin right, I guess, ended up with maggots crawling all over his legs."

LJ grinned, as if John had just described a gruesome scene in a horror movie.

"Developed gangrene or flesh-eating disease or something," John continued. "They might've been able to save him, by amputating, but what have we got to saw off a leg with?"

LJ laughed. Of course he did.

"Even if one of us did have the guts to try it."

6

The men were standing around a small fire. A pot of water was steaming on one of the rocks circling the firepit. There was a shabby lean-to near the tree line, and a pathetic attempt at a tent further up the beach.

"This is Ed," John said to LJ, nodding at Ed, whose face seemed permanently impassive, "and Anthony," Anthony nodded a welcome, "and Tim, Krush, and Biscuit," all younger men.

"Hey," LJ turned to Ed, "do you know how to hunt a rabbit and make—what's the word?" He looked at John for help.

"Cure," he said, smiling faintly.

"Yeah, and cure the skin right?"

Ed simply stared at him.

"Sure he does," Biscuit offered, cracking up. "They teach that in law school now."

The others grinned.

"You're a lawyer?"

Ed glared at him, accusing racism, then walked down to the water.

"I just meant—what's a lawyer doing in here?"

"We think he got a bit too aggressive defending land claims," Anthony said.

Biscuit, the consummate comic, let a beat pass before he added, "And we think it was this land." He burst into an infectious giggle. Pity he'd been exiled. He could've been Chris Rock meets Ellen DeGeneres.

"So you just got here?" Krush asked.

"Yeah. Yesterday," LJ said.

"Cool," Tim said. "Well, no, not cool," he glanced quickly at Anthony, "I mean—"

"Welcome," Biscuit said. "He means 'Welcome, to our beachside resort!' Over there," he gestured to the lean-to, "we have our cabana, which is at the moment—"

"We're heading out to do some fishing," Ed interrupted, having rejoined the group. He sent a warning glance Biscuit's way, then turned to LJ, "Would you like to come?"

"Nah, I think I'll just hang out here," he replied.

"Are you sure?" Anthony asked.

"Yeah, thanks, but my feet are still sore."

Ed shrugged. All of the men except Krush walked over to a large clump of bushes. John crawled in, then came back out with a fishing net of sorts. Biscuit crawled in next and came out with a woven basket and a spear. Then Ed, Tim, and Anthony reached in for their spears. They set out, walking along the beach away from the river, and Krush settled himself on the sand near the fire. LJ immediately joined him.

"This is the life, eh?" LJ said. "Lying on the beach in the sun."

Krush gave him an incredulous look, but didn't say anything.

"So what are you in for?" LJ tried again.

"You mean what am I out for."

"Yeah."

"I don't remember."

"Can't be all that long ago, how old are you, man?"

"Theft under, theft over, break and enter, assault, property damage. A whole bunch of stuff, but I don't remember any of it. I was blasted on somethin' or other."

"All three times?"

"Probably more than three."

"Guess there's no drugs here, huh."

"Oh, I didn't have a drug problem," Krush said, sarcastically. "John says I had RDD. Responsibility Deficit Disorder."

"Did you deal too?" LJ had missed the RDD bit.

"Yeah. I did. And before you ask, yeah, probably to kids. I dunno. Like I said. I don't remember."

LJ didn't pursue the matter. Instead, he got up, stretched, then pissed on the fire. As soon as Krush realized what he was doing, he jumped up in alarm, but it was too late—the fire was pretty much out. Krush desperately tried to salvage it, picking off the wet bits and blowing on a few embers, but to no avail.

"Fuck, man! What did you do that for?"

"What?"

"You put out the fuckin' fire! What's the matter with you?!"

"What's the big deal? Light another one."

"With what? You got some matches? A cigarette lighter maybe?"

LJ was silent as it sank in.

"You bring *any*thing?"

LJ looked confused.

"Fuck!" Krush was livid. He stamped around in the sand for a bit, then muttered, "Gotta go get my own damn fish now." He went to the large clump of bushes and pulled out a spear, as well as two sticks. He returned to LJ and threw the sticks at him. "Start rubbin'," he said angrily, then went off after the others. "Asshole," he added, just loudly enough for LJ to hear.

LJ looked at the sticks, sat down, then, since he had nothing better to do, started rubbing them together. Nothing happened. He persisted for about a minute then gave up.

A couple of hours later, the others returned, carrying, among them, three fish.

"Oh man, am I hungry!" LJ said, happy to see them.

Ed stopped in his tracks. "Did you help catch these fish?"

"Well, no, but—"

"Then what makes you think you should get to eat them?"

The others waited for his response. He was silent.

"If, however," Ed continued, "you'd kept the fire going, which was Krush's job—" He looked pointedly at Krush, who obviously wasn't in anyone's good books at the moment, "you would've been entitled. But as it is …" He headed down to the water with the fish.

"Well what am I supposed to eat?" LJ said petulantly to Ed's back.

Ed turned sharply to look at him. "How old are you?"

"Twenty— Hey, I'm fuckin' old enough!"

"Then act like it!"

Anthony picked up where Ed left off, but more gently. "You put the fire out. Did you start another one?" he asked, although it was clear to all that he hadn't.

"No, man, I tried, but—"

"Well, it's too late now to make a trip to the other side," John said, in a barely placating tone, "it'll be dark soon."

"Looks like it's sushi tonight," Anthony agreed.

"No way," Tim protested, "I ain't eatin' no raw fish."

"Like hell you aren't!" Anthony said angrily, almost as if he resented not just Tim's presence, but his very existence. "You put it in the lake for tomorrow, and it might not be there tomorrow! You're eating your fish tonight!"

"What I eat or don't eat ain't none of your business!" he retorted.

"Like hell it isn't!" Anthony responded. "After what I—"

"Yeah, well, I never asked—"

Both of them stopped short, each caught in a vicious circle that was apparently all too well worn. They just stood there for a moment, glaring at each other, then Anthony went down to the water to help Ed clean the fish.

"Why don't you and Krush go around to the other side tomorrow?" John said to LJ, trying to defuse the tension.

LJ looked at Krush, confused.

"There's usually some guys on the other side of the lake," Krush explained to LJ. "They keep a fire going too. Probably let us have some. And we never travel alone," he added.

"But I ain't got no shoes." LJ looked then at Biscuit, whose feet looked about the same size as his. "Hey man, can I borrow yours?"

"Hell no. I might never see 'em again. Can't have my Daffy Duck watch either, so don't even think 'bout askin'."

John stared at LJ with renewed disappointment. "You had all day, and you didn't make another fire *and* you didn't make any shoes?"

Ed had come back to the fire pit by this time, and stood beside John. LJ saw the disapproval in their faces.

"Hey, I don't need this shit," he said, and tried to stomp away, but in the sand, and with sore feet, he didn't pull it off. At all. He stopped. They all waited. Finally he turned.

"Okay, where do I get some of those weeds or whatever?"

John wordlessly headed toward the mucky area at the end of the river. LJ followed.

7

Early next morning, Krush nudged LJ awake, not very gently. "It's a long way around. We better get started."

LJ grunted, but got up. What he'd give for a long, hot shower. He shook the sand out of his clothes, then carefully put on the shoes he'd made the night before. They didn't look very promising.

LJ nodded to the knapsack Krush had put on. "Where'd you get that?"

"The dump."

"What dump?"

"There's a dump, left over from before, when people lived here. Other people," he corrected.

"Oh yeah, John mentioned that. Will we pass it? I'd like to check it out."

"We don't exactly pass it, it's kinda on the other side. We don't have time to stop anyway. But I can sort of show you where it is."

They headed out, walking along the beach, then past the point, around the mucky area, across the river, then along the shoreline.

"So what's up with Anthony and Tim?"

"No one knows exactly," Krush replied. "Feeling is—you know they're brothers, right?"

LJ shook his head.

"Well, they are, and the feeling is that whatever Anthony did, or confessed to doing, he did to keep his kid brother from getting sent here."

"And he ended up here anyway."

"Yeah. And you should hear him sing. Anthony. Man,

he coulda been somethin'."

"So what did Tim do? To get sent here?"

"Dunno."

A short while later, during which it became clear LJ's shoes were not going to make the trip, the shoreline became an impenetrable forest.

"Now what?" LJ said. As if it were Krush's fault the way was blocked.

"Now we go through there," Krush nodded to a barely discernible path through the trees, managing to ignore LJ's tone. "So we'll be away from the lake for a while."

He took an empty plastic bottle from his knapsack and filled it with water from the lake. They each drank as much as they could, then Krush filled the bottle once more and put it back in his knapsack.

"Sometimes we hear wolves or coyotes or something in this area," Krush said, a little nervously, "but not until it gets dark."

"Hey, look!" LJ cried out in delight about an hour later. The forest had become less dense, and they'd come upon a couple of apple trees. Whether the deciduous forest was moving north due to the climate change or whether the trees were the remnants of someone's attempt at an apple orchard, they had no way of knowing. Probably the former, since they'd discovered apple trees at a few locations. LJ reached out for the nearest apple.

"No!" Krush shouted. "Only the ripest one. Leave the others. They'll be good later." He looked around on the ground, while LJ looked up at the tree, then started climbing.

"Here's one," Krush called up a moment later.

LJ looked down. "It looks half-rotten," he said with some distaste. "There's a better one up here."

"You can eat around the rotten part," Krush said. "But take that one too. Maybe you can trade it for some fish tonight."

LJ picked the apple, then started climbing back down. When he jumped to the ground, one of his shoes fell apart.

"Fuck!" He kicked at what was left of his shoe. More than once. "This is shit! This is all fucking shit!" FUCK this SHIT!"

Krush waited until his anger had passed, grinning at LJ's extensive vocabulary.

"Are you done? Can we carry on now?"

"I *can't* carry on!" LJ protested.

"Suck it up, man." He turned his back to LJ and started walking.

LJ stood there. Between a rock and a hard place.

"Hold up!" he shouted, then rushed to catch up.

Krush turned, traded the rotten apple he'd picked up for the good one LJ still had, against all odds, in his hand. He stowed it safely in his knapsack, then continued walking.

LJ limped along behind, wearing just the one shoe, chewing around the rotten part of the apple. A miserable two-year-old. A few minutes later, he tossed the remaining rotten apple away.

"Hey, don't just throw it away!" Krush went after it, looked around a bit, selected a spot, then planted the seeds. "If we're lucky, it'll grow and we'll have another apple tree here some day."

Half a mile later, Krush picked up some dry twigs and put them in his knapsack. "We'll need these on the way back," he said. "Look for really dry, really small bits."

After another half a mile, they stopped for a short rest. Krush took out the water bottle, drank half of it, then offered the rest to LJ. LJ drained the bottle, then tossed it into the bush.

"Hey!" Krush went after the bottle, retrieving it like it was a treasure. Which of course it was. "What the fuck are you doing? You gotta stop tossing shit away!"

"Sorry, man. I wasn't thinking."

"Gotta stop doin' that too."

"There's a wide open stretch ahead," Krush said, a long and difficult hour later, "and then another bit of bush, then we're on the other side." LJ just grunted. His feet were bruised and scraped.

Suddenly they heard some shouts. Surprised, they froze, and through the thinning trees, saw a small pack of men attack two other men, no doubt newcomers. Krush reached out to stop LJ from running out to assist. Found it was unnecessary. One of the newcomers fell to the onslaught. Fell hard. The other hesitated, then took off, screaming "911! Someone call 911!"

As if the chase was more fun, the pack took off after the second newcomer. Krush and LJ quickly ran out then, but it was clear the fallen man was already dead. His head had been bashed in with a rock.

Krush nodded toward his feet. LJ looked at him, a little repulsed, but after just a moment's hesitation, started untying the laces.

"Hurry it up," Krush said nervously, glancing around, "in case we have to run for it. They may be coming back for those."

It was early afternoon by the time they arrived at the other side of the lake. Three men, all looking like they'd been wearing the same clothes for months, which of course they had, were huddled near a small fire.

"Hey, Bob," Krush nodded to all three, who nodded back.

"Hey Krush, how's it goin'?"

"Good, man. How's it goin' here?"

"Oh, well, you know."

"Yeah. This is LJ. He's new."

"Hey."

"So, we, ah—"

"Your fire went out."

"Yeah."

"But it was my fault," LJ spoke up.

Krush looked surprised at LJ's rush to claim responsibility.

"Uh-huh," Bob simply said. Then added, "Yeah, sure, help yourself."

Krush unpacked two odd little box structures from his knapsack, each with a bunch of small stones in them, then went about carefully transferring embers from the fire into the little boxes.

"Some dry stuff over there," Bob nodded.

Krush went to the pile Bob indicated and added some dry leaves and bits of twig to the boxes, blowing until there was a little flame in each. Then he handed one to LJ.

"Careful with it now!" he said. "Don't jiggle the stones on the bottom, keep it sheltered from the wind, and watch it. You gotta feed it to keep it going all the way back. But not too much or the box will burn."

"Why do we need two?"

"Because one's going to go out."

"Or two," Bob said, grinning. "We'll be here."

"Yeah. Hate to chat and rush, but—"

"It'll be dark soon enough even if you don't have to come back."

With no further ado, they left the way they came, carefully holding their fireboxes.

"So what are those guys here for?" LJ asked, as they walked along. It was slow going through the bush with their fireboxes.

"Don't know the other two guys, never seen 'em before, but Bob—he says he didn't pay child support."

"That's a crime?"

Krush stopped short at that, and LJ bumped into him.

"Damn!"

"Went out?" Krush asked.

"Yeah, sorry, man."

"Well we still got one. Let's keep going. Pick up dry leaves and stuff as you go. And you go first, keep the wind off me."

"Hey Krush, LJ," Bob said, chuckling. "Long time no see. There's a couple big embers there on the left."

Krush went through the same routine.

Again they left the way they came. Again carefully holding their fireboxes.

It was late afternoon.

"We really have to stop meeting this way."

"Tell me about it."

As they approached the spot where they saw the attack, LJ broke their silence. "So what's the story with—"

"The beaters? That's what we call 'em. We figure a lot of 'em are here for beatin' on their women. And it seems they can't live without beatin' on someone— Hey, watch where you're going!"

"Sorry. Still good?"

"Yeah."

It was early evening by the time they made it to the shore on their side of the lake. LJ's fire had long gone out, and the last mile had been painstakingly slow, their only light, the little fire in Krush's box.

"Just a little further man," LJ encouraged, "we're almost there."

"Can't see my fuckin' feet in this fuckin' dark," Krush said, walking like he was carrying nitroglycerine. "You tell me when there's something I'm gonna trip over."

"Yeah, you're doin' good. The mucky part's just ahead."

A long fifteen minutes later, they got within view of the beach.

"Hey, they got a fire!"

He ran ahead to the strong blaze.

"Doesn't hurt to have two," Krush muttered to himself. "Just in case. Came all this fuckin' way."

"You got fire!" LJ yelled at John, who was closest. Ed and a stranger were standing on the other side. Anthony, Tim, and Biscuit were just coming up from the water, one of them carrying the small pot, the others carrying the day's catch.

"Thought you didn't have any matches or nothin'!" He was enraged. "So why the fuck did we go through all that then?" He swung his arms about, vaguely gesticulating. All that work! Twice they'd had to go back—

"Henry did it," John said evenly.

LJ was still thrashing about, "Well if it was that easy, why the fuck—"

"Who said it was easy?" John stared at LJ. "Henry?"

Henry walked around to John and LJ.

"Show him your hands."

Henry opened his hands in the light of the fire. They were raw and blistered.

LJ was confused. "But why? We went over to the other side. You knew that."

"We weren't sure you'd make it back. With fire."

They were all suddenly silent, respectful, as Krush arrived with his pathetic little flame in a box.

He set his little fire in the sand beside the big one, then turned to Henry. "My fire's bigger than your fire."

They both started to giggle, silly with exhaustion. They sat down then to admire their efforts, Krush collapsing with the release of miles of tension, Henry sitting with his hands, limp, palms up, in his lap.

"Time for a fish fry!" Anthony said, skewering onto long sticks filets of the fish they'd caught and cleaned that afternoon.

"Yeah!" Tim agreed enthusiastically, passing the sticks around. As they settled themselves around the fire to fry their fish, LJ got his apple out of Krush's knapsack.

"I didn't help catch the fish, so—but I've got an apple—" He felt like an idiot, and glanced at Krush, who nodded encouragement. "Does anyone want to trade me this apple for a fish?"

They all stared at him.

"Sure thing," Biscuit broke the silence. "Here you go. One fish-on-a-stick for one apple."

"Thanks, man."

LJ made a spot for himself in the sand and extended his

fish into the fire, while Biscuit made a show of polishing the apple before he put it in his pocket.

"Anyone got a bag of Doritos to trade?" he asked. " I got another fish-on-a-stick here—"

Krush and Tim groaned. This teasing mention of the many foods they craved was not new.

"You found some shoes," John commented, nodding at LJ's feet as he filled his mug with a cup of hot water from the pot.

"Yeah."

Krush told them what had happened. "We didn't have time to salvage anything else. Had to leave the body for the animals."

"And they say it tastes like chicken," Biscuit said with a broad grin. More groans.

LJ remembered then that the newcomer had been wearing a sweatshirt. That must've been what Krush had in mind. "So what do you guys do when it gets cold?" he asked, staring at the fire, waiting for his fish to fry.

"Shiver," Biscuit said.

"Build bigger fires," Krush said.

The fish filets were soon cooked, and there wasn't much talk while they ate. Occasionally someone would go down to the lake to refill the pot.

"No one's ever got sick from drinking the lake water?" LJ had been drinking it all day, but the thought just occurred to him.

"Not that we know of," John spoke, sticking his now-empty skewer in the sand. "You should talk to Ike. He knows a lot of what's happened. You know, history."

"I ain't interested in no history."

"Oh, well, then," John said, miffed, and disappointed, at LJ's rejection. Of knowledge.

"What are you interested in?" Ed asked, not too kindly.

LJ had missed the meaning of John's reply, and Ed's tone confused him. Had he been asking too many questions?

"Nothin' I guess."

A little while later, LJ tried again, uncomfortable with the quiet. "Hey, John, what did you mean before—about the taxes? When you said it'd be different if it was just *some* taxes. That you didn't pay."

"Well," John said, "I guess I meant that that would be breaking the law for a legitimate reason. You know, there are good laws and bad laws. Breaking the bad ones, that's just civil disobedience. And maybe, I don't know, but maybe it wouldn't've counted for the ThreeStrike."

"You mean some crimes count and some don't?" Biscuit said. That was news to him. "How is that fair?"

"You think all crimes are the same?" Ed asked, always interested in a good debate.

"Well … no."

"So what crimes do you think should count for the ThreeStrike?" He asked.

"And what should be done about the other crimes?" John added.

"Murder," Tim suggested. "Killing someone is definitely wrong."

"Even in self-defence?" Ed asked.

"Okay, no, but otherwise."

"But what if it was an accident?" Krush spoke up. "What if you didn't intend to kill someone? What if you didn't even *know* that you killed someone?"

"They still die," Anthony said, gently, recognizing that Krush was probably talking about himself.

"Yeah." Krush admitted. And continued scratching aimlessly in the sand with his skewer stick.

"So we have to decide whether it's the consequence or the intent that matters," Ed said.

“What do you mean ‘we’?” LJ asked, feeling like he was missing something.

Ed glanced at John before answering. “Hypothetically. If you were running the place. If you were trying to create a society—”

“But there’s accidents and then there’s accidents,” Tim said.

Anthony looked at him, encouraging him to continue.

“Like there’s accidents that you should’ve known better and then there’s just, like, accidents.”

“Negligence,” Ed supplied the word. “Young Tim just described the legal concept of negligence. When you should’ve known better, when you can reasonably foresee the consequences, and you do it anyway, you’re negligent.”

“And guilty,” John added.

“Okay,” LJ said, “and what about the small stuff—that’s not an accident?”

“Like just stealing shit?” Biscuit said.

“Yeah.”

“Well, you’re taking something that doesn’t belong to you,” Anthony said. “That’s wrong, isn’t it?”

“Ah, but define ‘belong,’” Ed said. “Stealing someone’s car would be a clear case of theft. But what about taking something that you think belonged to you in the first place?”

“That’d be like taking back stolen goods,” Tim suggested. “No crime in that.”

“Or like not paying income tax?” Biscuit looked at John. “It’s your money, you earned it, how is it wrong if you just keep it?”

“Because I used the roads without paying for them,” John said. “So it’s like I stole the use of them.”

“But you didn’t actually steal the roads,” Tim said. Biscuit giggled, imagining how one could go about stealing a road. “So how can that be wrong?”

"Think of it like downloading music off the internet without permission," Ed said. "You don't steal the song, but you steal the use of it."

"But are they both wrong?" Biscuit asked.

"Suppose you spend a day working for a man," Ed replied, "fixing his roof, say, then he doesn't pay you. He hasn't stolen you—"

"But he's stolen the use of you," Tim got it.

"He's taken your labor without paying," Anthony added, casting a glance at LJ. Who got it too. Now.

Long after the men had fallen silent, Tim started to sing, softly, "'I'm ridin' in your car, you turn on the radio.'" It was a question.

Biscuit answered, with the next line. "'You're pullin' me close, I just say no.'"

LJ looked around, not quite sure what was going on. John and Henry exchanged a smile.

"'I say I don't like it, but you know I'm a liar,'" Krush sang the next line.

Then Anthony's voice—ached, "''Cause when we kiss, oh—'"

"'Fire.'" In perfect four-part harmony.

Henry smiled at LJ and gestured a small 'ta-dah': "Introducing: Rapacapella!"

LJ was delighted then as the four of them broke into a rhythmic, swinging, half-rap, a capella version of the Pointer Sisters' song. He tapped a quiet back-up beat on his legs.

It was a fine way to end the day. All things considered.

8

Several days later, during which the men spent their time gathering firewood, having to go further and further each day for it, fishing, repairing sandals, working on the tent, or the lean-to, or digging a pit—Ed had an idea about living underground during the winter—LJ wandered off to walk along the shore. Tim, Biscuit, and Krush watched him with curiosity as he looked intently at the water line. Occasionally, he'd bend down and feel the sand.

"That's not how you fish," Biscuit said and got the hoped-for laugh.

When LJ returned to the group, Tim asked him what he had been doing.

"Looking for clay. Thought I might figure out how to make a mug. Like yours."

"First, I got mine at the dump."

"And second," John had joined them, "someone already tried that."

"Then why didn't you tell me?" LJ was angry. "I told you what I was going to do, when I wandered off and you said I shouldn't go too far by myself."

"You said you weren't interested in history," he replied. "That's history."

Early that afternoon, a stranger appeared, holding up his hands up as he approached. He stopped about thirty feet away, as was the established etiquette in cases like this. The men gathered to face him.

"Someone named LJ here?"

"Yeah," LJ replied. "Who wants to know?"

The others looked at him harshly.

"There's someone at the window asking for you."

"What window?"

"There's a place in the wall where the forcefield is weak or somethin'," Krush said, standing nearest to him. "You can hear someone on the other side if they're real close."

"And someone's there? Now?"

"Apparently," Biscuit said, excited. "And asking for you! Are you famous or what?"

"All right!" LJ cheered. "I am getting *out* of here!" He turned to the man. "Can you show me this window? Can you take me there? How far is it?"

"'Bout two hours," he said, and started walking away. "Come on."

LJ hurriedly put on his new shoes—John had suggested he wear them only when necessary, to make them last—then ran to catch up.

The stranger kept ahead of LJ the whole way, making no attempt to befriend or converse. LJ found that a bit odd and wondered if he were being set up for another attack, but surely the guys at the beach would have told him. Unless that was history too.

After what was indeed about two hours, the man simply pointed to the left. And took off to the right.

LJ approached the spot the man had pointed to.

"Hello? K? Dub?"

"Hello?" It was a stranger's voice.

"Who's there?" LJ moved a bit to the left, then to the right, trying to find—

"Is that LJ?"

"Yeah." He could hear clearly now. "Who are you?"

"I'm Mr. Morgan."

"I don't know no Mr. Morgan." LJ turned away in disgust. And anger. But what else was new.

Where the fuck was K? Why wasn't he getting him out of this hell-hole?

"I pick up—I picked up your garbage twice a week. On your street, where you lived."

"Yeah? I never saw you." LJ had turned back.

Mr. Morgan sighed. "I know." LJ had never seen anyone but himself.

"So what are you doing here? It's not exactly in the neighbourhood. You here to get me out?"

"No, I'm afraid I can't do that."

LJ turned away again.

"You don't think you belong there?"

And turned back again.

"There's nothin' here!" LJ spat out the words. "What'd I do to deserve this? I didn't kill no one! I ain't done nothin'—"

"What *did* you do? The first time." Mr. Morgan knew very well what LJ had done.

"I knocked over some garbage cans. Big deal."

"And wrecked Mrs. Emerson's garden."

"Yeah. So? Didn't mean nothin'."

"It meant something to Mrs. Emerson. That was her husband's garden, and when he died, she spent all of her time there, tending it, taking care of it. She loved that garden like, like it was him. Cried for days when she saw what you'd done to it."

"Yeah, well, tell her I'm sorry," he said. Not at all sorry.

"And it took me an extra two hours to pick up the garbage that day. Missed my granddaughter's first piano recital."

"So for that I get sent here? I was just a kid."

"You were fifteen," Mr. Morgan didn't quite agree. "And the second time?" he asked after a moment.

"That was an accident."

"How can you get drunk by accident? Tell me."

LJ was silent. If he'd thought— If he'd realized that everything he'd ever said was either kneejerk, or defensive, or denial …

"How can you steal a car," Mr. Morgan persisted, "and then when you're finished with your little joyride, just leave it in the middle of the road—how do you do that by accident?"

"I thought it was the side of the road. I was drunk, okay?"

"Oh and that excuses you? You chose to drink that much. Are you saying you didn't know what happens when you drink that much?"

LJ didn't say anything.

"The family coming around the corner didn't have a chance. That poor child will spend the rest of her life in a wheelchair."

"Yeah, well, that's not my fault."

"Then whose fault is it?" Mr. Morgan might've shouted. But he really wanted to hear LJ's answer.

"I didn't mean for that to happen, okay?! That wasn't supposed to happen!"

"Oh well then," Mr. Morgan said, a little sarcastically, "what did you *mean* to happen when you left the car in the middle of the road? What was *supposed to* happen? Are you saying other people aren't supposed to be using the road when you're using it? Who the hell are you?"

"How did I know they'd be coming around the corner?"

"What, you didn't know people drive cars on roads—around corners?"

"I still don't deserve this," LJ muttered. "Can't a man change?"

"You're what," Mr. Morgan replied, "twenty-three? Twenty-three years old and running through the subway with complete disregard for others. For what matters to them. When were you planning to change? What exactly were you waiting for?"

"Look, Mr.—" LJ had already forgotten his name, "why did you come here? What do you want?"

"What do I want?" Mr. Morgan turned away and stared out at the distance. Truthfully, he didn't quite know. "What do *you* want?"

"I don't want nothin'!"

"Well, I guess you got what you want then."

They were both silent.

After a moment, Mr. Morgan tried again. "I just thought—all those years ago, I thought maybe if I'd said something—"

"Yeah and what might that have been? You're a fucking garbageman."

"What's that supposed to mean?" Now it was his turn to be angry. "You think you're too good to pick up other people's garbage? To cut the grass at the city's parks? Repair the roads? Tell me, what job do you think is appropriate for a person of your skills and abilities?"

LJ said nothing.

"At least I pay my way." Mr. Morgan turned and started to walk away, so LJ barely heard his next words. "And I'm tired of payin' yours too."

But heard them he did. "What's that supposed to mean?" LJ hollered after him. "You didn't pay nothin' of mine!"

Mr. Morgan returned to the window.

"Like hell I didn't! For starters, your rehab, and then your time in prison—who do you think pays for that?"

"Hey, I worked when I was in prison!"

"It costs $300 a day to keep a man in prison. You say you worked, you figure you earned your keep? You earned $300 a day? Tell me, what did you do that was so very difficult, or so very dangerous, or so very valuable, it was worth $300 a day?"

LJ was silent. He hadn't done the math. Of course he hadn't.

Mr. Morgan began to leave again.

"Are you leavin'?" LJ called out, threatening. "We ain't done yet!"

Mr. Morgan stopped and turned.

"No, we aren't," he agreed. Then sighed. "But do you really want me to come back?"

"It's not like I've got anything better to do," LJ mumbled. After a long pause.

"Well then, maybe I'll be here again next week."

9

After Mr. Morgan left, LJ sat at the window for quite a while. Thinking. Trying to think.

Pity morality is typically conveyed as a matter of rules. Rules presented, by both parents and teachers, as stand-alones. Without any attached reasoning. And, further, as things to be broken if you're a *real* man. Which is the goal of any self-respecting male. So no wonder.

Eventually, suddenly cognizant of being maybe two hours away from the others, away from help, should he need it, he figured he should start back.

And only then realized he hadn't been paying enough attention to landmarks … He hadn't been paying *any* attention to landmarks …

After three hours, he saw in the far distance the hill with one lone tree on top that Krush had pointed out as the location, more or less, of the dump. Well, he had nothing better to do with the rest of the day, maybe he could find a mug or a water bottle he could clean out.

John was right. It had been thoroughly picked over. There were heaps and humps of stuff, but as far as he could tell, it was all useless. But what the hell, he was here, he may as well take a *good* look. At first he started rummaging with his hands, gingerly, but then it occurred to him that he'd be better off poking around with a stick. Maybe there was *something* useful buried under the crap.

So he went to the bush circling of the dump, found a poking stick, returned, and started digging around. All the organic stuff had long decomposed, but there were pieces of vinyl, and metal, all bent and twisted … He found a lot of plastic bags, but every one of them was filthy and torn, nothing he could clean and tape together, should he find tape … He became excited about one large bag of something, but when he opened it up, he realized it was, had been, a bundle of soiled disposable diapers… He turned up his nose, even though the smell was long gone, and hurled it far away … He did find several grungy plastic bottles, but every one of them was cracked, and none had caps …

In the meantime, Ed, John, Anthony, Tim, Krush, and Biscuit were sitting around the fire.

"Well, what say we all? Is he in or is he not?" Ed opened the discussion.

"I say he's in," Krush cast his vote. "He stuck it out that whole way to get fire."

"Yeah, but he pissed it out in the first place," John countered. "And didn't you say he tossed the apple, then the water bottle?"

"Sat here all day and didn't even try to make shoes for himself," Anthony offered, "let alone a fire."

"I know, I know," Krush conceded. "But he reminds me of me, not so long ago. He'll come around."

"He could've taken off on you," Tim noted, "but he didn't. I say he's in too."

"Okay, but what can he do?" John countered. "What does he bring to the group?"

"He became decidedly volatile when he discovered that his trip around the lake was for nothing," Ed said. "That makes me nervous."

"Decidedly nervous?" Biscuit wanted to ask, but his timing was better than that. "I like him," he said instead. "I say he's in."

"Anthony?" Ed asked.

"I don't know. I want to say yes, but…"

A long while later, LJ finally found his way back.

"Arranged your escape?" John asked, not too kindly, as LJ walked up to the fire.

LJ just scowled. He'd been such a fool. If there was a way out, wouldn't these guys have found it by now?

"No," he admitted. "But I found these at the dump. I figure they could belong to the group."

John took the pair of kids' scissors from his outstretched hand.

"You're giving these to us?" He examined the scissors. "Thank you! These will really come in handy!" He smiled at him. For perhaps the first time. Then he looked pointedly at Ed and Anthony.

"It's just scissors," LJ said. "*Kids'* scissors."

"Which means they're perfect for us," Biscuit said. "We best make sure we don't run with 'em."

Next morning, everyone was closely huddled around the fire, as usual. They'd long given up their homophobia for warmth.

"So, anyone goin' fishin' today?" LJ asked. "I'd like to go along."

Anthony looked at him. "Yeah? That's good."

"But we—" John said.

"But first, there is—" Ed said at the same time, then gave way to John. They weren't fighting over who would be leader; both were smart enough to realize that would be stupid. It's just that they were both used to filling that role.

"We have something to tell you first," John continued, with a slight nod to Ed.

LJ looked a little concerned.

"You're in."

"In what?" he asked, uncertainly.

"Well, we've got a group, sort of," John explained, "we're trying to make a go of this—"

"And we vote on new people," Anthony continued, "to see if we want them, to see if we trust them—"

"You mean this was a test?" LJ asked. "I've been doing some sort of a test?"

"Yeah," Krush said. "First you failed."

"Then you passed," Biscuit said. "Then you failed. Then you passed."

"But I'm in?" LJ looked from one to the other. "I passed?"

John looked a little uncomfortable. "Well, most of us think you passed. So we're going to take you to the cabin tomorrow."

LJ was still processing the news about the vote.

"There's a cabin?" he finally said.

"There's a couple, actually," John explained. "Hunters' cabins, by the look of them, from before. And we've sort of appropriated one of them. You'll see."

"Okay. Okay! Thanks, man," LJ had finally sorted it out. What they'd said. How he felt about it. "Everyone, I mean. Thanks."

10

After burying their fishing gear in the sand and packing what few personal possessions they had in the communal knapsack Krush had worn for their trip across the lake, they headed out to the cabin the next morning.

"So who was at the window?" Krush asked LJ. They were all curious.

"Some guy from before. Says he's the garbageman from our street."

"What'd he want?" Tim asked.

"Don't really know. Rag on me a bit." Suddenly LJ hit his head. "Damn! I shoulda asked him if he had any matches!"

"It wouldn't've mattered," Anthony had been listening. "He couldn't've given them to you anyway. Nothing physical can get through the field."

"Krush tried to throw a rock through the wall once," Biscuit offered, grinning broadly.

"Hey!" Krush didn't want to hear this story.

But LJ did. "Yeah? What happened?"

"It bounced back," Biscuit said. "Hit him in the head." He giggled, and Krush playfully shoved him, looking a little embarrassed. LJ laughed, but not in a mean way. He would've tried the exact same thing at some point.

They walked on without talking for a bit.

"So do any of you meet anyone at the window?" LJ asked. "I mean, you could, right?"

There was an awkward silence. Ed pointedly walked on ahead. Anthony looked at Tim, just at the moment Tim looked at Anthony—they were each other's only family.

Anthony was pleased that Tim had looked his way, even though he hadn't actually smiled; Tim didn't know quite what to make of the moment. Krush and Biscuit both looked off into the distance. No one had ever come to ask for them. It hurt.

"My wife wanted to," John broke the silence. "But I told her not to. She's got to get on with her life. Best if it's a clean cut. I may as well be dead." He looked out at the sky. "And it hurts too much," he confessed. "Maintaining contact." He nodded slightly toward Ed, "Especially if there's kids."

"You know," John had caught up with Ed, "we really should set up some sort of safe passage gate at the doors. At least the one that's closest to us."

Ed grunted.

"Think of all the stuff we might then have access to. All the stuff newcomers might bring."

Ed grunted.

"Ed, you're being taciturn."

He smiled slightly. "LJ didn't bring any stuff."

"LJ probably didn't know he could bring stuff."

Ed grunted. "Or maybe he just assumed that his needs would be taken care of by others."

It was John's turn to grunt.

A moment later he asked, "Did you? Bring stuff?"

"Yes," Ed said, "even though my arrest was—unexpected. I went straight from custody to court to the escort van. My wife had two hours to put something together."

They walked on.

"She didn't think to pack a survival handbook," he said ruefully, wistfully, "but still, she did well. Some of the stuff at the cabin is stuff she packed," Ed said. "You?"

"Oh I saw it coming. And I was ready. In addition to

my smartphone—which is why *I* didn't think to pack a survival handbook—don't know *why* I thought there'd be cell towers in exile—I had a pack full of camping gear: a Swiss army knife, a first aid kit, a tent, a sleeping bag, winter clothes—and two pairs of shoes. But I met the same fate as LJ. If there'd been someone there to meet me—"

"There was." Ed almost grinned. John laughed.

"I even had a flint stick," John said. Ed's eyebrows rose. "And a hole in my pocket," he sighed. "Spent two weeks retracing my steps trying to find it."

They didn't know, but would have guessed, that most men brought fifty pounds of weaponry with them. Fortunately—or unfortunately, given the presence of bears and deer—most of them used all the ammo they'd brought in the first week.

Ed would have thought to have brought a hunting rifle, but that also hadn't occurred to his wife. She wouldn't've had time to get one, legally, in any case.

No doubt the beaters beat each other up over knives. John still had his Swiss army knife—in fact, they regularly used it to 'clean' their fish—but he never carried it with him. It was too precious to lose and if he ever tried to use it as a weapon, it would most likely end up being used against him. He had no idea how to fight with a knife. He had no idea how to fight, really.

"You didn't get mugged upon entry?" John asked after a moment.

"I was part of a group. There were six of us. Shortly after we passed through, we saw a couple people in the distance, but we didn't know then what the situation was… I guess they thought the better of it."

"No doubt."

"And the other guys who arrived with you?"

"Four of them took off. Tapper and I stayed together."

"I didn't know you and Tapper came together," John

said, surprised.

Ed just nodded.

"Didn't Anthony say he arrived with others? They took off as well, I guess. I remember he said he'd brought his iPod, a solar charger, and headphones. Said he didn't need anything else."

They both smiled. Sadly. Anthony had never told anyone what had happened to his precious iPod. Or to him, presumably. Since he wouldn't've given it up without a struggle of some sort.

About an hour later, Ed spoke. "When I left, the prison population in Canada was twenty-three percent First Nations. Even with all the imports from the States, many of my people must still be coming here, and without the booze, they could be sober long enough to discover the men they were intended to be—"

John immediately saw where he was going. "You want to set up a brand new Cherokee nation!"

"Mohawk, but— If there were several of us, a small band, we could leave, head north, try to find our ancestral lands, rediscover the ancient ways …"

"Form a new League of Nations."

"You know your history."

John simply nodded. They walked on.

"Does the genetic heritage really matter that much to you?" John asked after a long while. He was surprised. He knew Ed was an activist about First Nations issues, but surely anyone as intelligent and as rational as he was …

"Anthony is a good man," John continued. "So are the others. Mostly. I might even want to join your League," he added.

Ed didn't reply.

A little hurt by that, John tried then to make light of

the matter. "Well, it *is* your land—"

"It *is* our land!" Ed insisted with sudden vehemence. "And you—"

"Hey, not *me*—I wasn't even born yet!"

"No, but you've inherited the privilege that—" Ed suddenly stopped. It was an old argument. A tired argument.

"Are you sure it's your land?" John was curious. "All of it?"

"Don't worry, my friend. We'll set up a preserve so the White Man can live out his years."

John opened his mouth to correct 'preserve' but then realized that as a lawyer, Ed would have been choosing his words carefully. He glanced sideways but Ed's face was inscrutable. Hard to see if he'd been kidding.

"The beaters may have already established a nation," John said a while later. He and Ed were still walking together in the lead, but the others were close enough behind for safety. Or at least, hopefully, deterrence. "Hell, they could be occupying half a dozen solar-fitted summer homes on a beautiful lake somewhere...

"And maybe they're making organized raids on newcomers—maybe the beaters we see out and about are just outliers, renegades ...

"Which means maybe they have *lots* of stuff— All the survival books and tools everyone ever thought to bring...

"In fact," John continued his line of thought as they continued walking, "that might be why they haven't come after us. Have they ever raided the cabin?"

Ed shook his head.

"Maybe what *we* have is small potatoes to them—" He grinned then. "What I'd give for a small potato ..."

A while later, after he finished thinking about small potatoes, John thought about an alliance with the beaters.

But he quickly rejected the idea. He thought about trade. Rejected the idea. The only relationship likely to develop was war. He sighed.

After about four hours, they arrived at the cabin. It was indeed an old hunter's cabin. It had been, at one time, efficiently functional. Not luxurious by any means, but well-kept. Now it had the appearance of having been stripped, and to some extent, trashed. Four of the five windows had no glass or screen. The door hung lopsided, one of its hinges pulled out of the frame. The chimney was missing its cap. And instead of wood stacked all neat and tidy in the adjoining lean-to, there was a pile of odd shaped chunks, many of which looked too large to fit into a stove.

As they approached, LJ heard voices. "Someone's already there," he said in a low voice.

"Yeah," John said, "we take turns. The cabin's not big enough for everyone—though that's one of our projects—building an addition or something—so we take turns. One group lives here for a week, the other lives out, and then we switch."

Henry came out of the cabin and stood on the top step.

"Hey, Ed, John." He nodded at the others, then acknowledged LJ. "New guy. I see you're in."

"Yeah."

"Okay. Welcome. A tour?"

Henry looked inquiringly at Ed and John, and got an affirmative response. From John. Ed abstained. So he led LJ to the side of the cabin, the others tagging along.

"Our firewood supply," Henry nodded into the lean-to.

"And," as they rounded the corner to the back, "Our garden!" He nodded to a patch of dirt

Tapper, looking of all the men the most comfortable

with the survival-in-the-wild thing, had heard them arrive and was up off his knees, standing in the middle of the patch.

"Hey, good to see you!" he smiled at the group, then turned to LJ, "Hey."

LJ nodded back.

"There's not much in it at the moment," Tapper explained to LJ, "because we can't exactly go to Levitt's Feed and Seed. But apparently it was a garden at some point in time, and *something's* growing. We're just not quite sure what yet. Nor are we sure what to do about it."

"We water it!" Biscuit said, nodding to the pump handle barely visible on the far side of the patch. "We're sure about that much. 'Cuz we're rocket scientists."

Thirsty, LJ started to walk toward the pump.

"Hey!" Tapper yelled.

LJ stopped, puzzled.

"Watch where you're walking!"

"Oh." LJ looked down at his feet. He had made a direct line toward the pump. Right through the patch.

Tapper looked darkly at the John, Ed, and the others.

"You don't make a move here without someone telling you," he continued to scold LJ, "without someone showing you. Not one move, d'ya hear?"

"Okay, got it, no need to—"

"No, he's right," John said firmly to LJ. "You don't do anything without permission, without guidance. We don't have a lot of room for error."

"Or carelessness," Anthony added.

"It would serve you right if Tapper never let you eat *any* of the food he grows," Ed said.

"He can't do that!" LJ protested.

"Oh?" Ed asked archly. "And why not?"

"It wouldn't be fair!" Lame. And he knew it.

"Fair? *Fair?*" Ed repeated in disbelief. "Do you even *lis-*

ten to yourself? What's not fair about it?"

Suddenly there were sounds of a fight from inside the cabin. Anthony raced around to the door, quickly followed by Henry. The others followed, John and Tapper only after making sure LJ carefully retraced his steps backwards out of the garden.

A moment later, both Anthony and Henry came out of the cabin, forcibly restraining a third man, Carlos, who was shouting and struggling. They led him past the others some distance away from the cabin, but still held on.

"I'm sick of it!" the man was shouting and struggling against their hold on him. "We got nothin' here! Can't even have a smoke! And I'm just sick and tired of it! I'm—I'm just sick and tired…" His shouting turned quickly to weeping, and when they released him, he just fell to his knees. "All I want is a lousy cigarette. A hamburger. Some clean clothes."

Another man, Juan, came out to stand in the doorway.

"The dishes are plastic, thank God, but our only pot doesn't have a handle anymore. And—" He held up a broken CD player.

"No," Anthony said, stepping toward Juan. He took the player from him, gently. And tried not to cry. It had been—

Ed looked at LJ then. "We can't afford anger either. You feel a tantrum coming on, you get the hell away from everything and everyone, you got that?"

LJ nodded, then spoke quietly. "You had a CD player?"

"Yeah," Krush answered, quietly, "and the good thing, one of the very few good things here, is that it didn't need batteries."

"Solar-powered," Tim explained, going to stand beside Anthony. It was all he could do.

"Maybe we can fix it. I could—" LJ trailed off, eager to please but—

"Yeah?" John asked hopefully. "You know about electronics?"

He looked down sheepishly. "Well, no."

"Then you don't touch it," Ed said, firmly. "We'll wait for someone who knows what they're doing. Bound to be someone, sooner or later." He put his hand on Anthony's shoulder.

"So what exactly *can* I do?" LJ muttered, mostly to himself, once Juan had gone back inside, followed by Tapper and Ed.

"Well, you tell us."

LJ looked at John, unsure if that was a challenge or a sincere question.

John looked at Carlos, still in a heap some distance from the cabin, then he looked at Henry. "Continue the tour," he said.

Henry led LJ around to the back of the cabin again, the rest of them tagging along, dispiritedly. They made a wide detour around the garden.

"Here we have our livestock," he pointed to two rabbits in a makeshift chicken wire cage on his left, and a grouse in another cage on the right. "The idea is that, well, you know what rabbits do best—we're hoping eventually we'll have great quantities of rabbit stew—and whatever else we can manage."

"Rabbitskin clothes." As soon as he said it—

"Well, we have to figure that one out," Henry said. "You should talk to Ike. In the meantime, unfortunately, what we have here is two boy bunnies."

"Hey, I didn't know," Tim protested.

"'Course you didn't," Henry said. "Not criticizing."

"Tim's the one who caught those for us," Anthony said proudly.

"Really?" LJ was impressed. "All right!" He high-fived him.

"Used to play basketball," Tim grinned. "Guard. I'm fast and good at zigzagging."

"And the bird. Does it lay eggs?" LJ asked.

"Well—"

"Tim seems to have a little sexual confusion going on," Biscuit grinned.

"Do not!" They scuffled for a bit, laughing.

"Well, that's it for here," Henry concluded the tour, leading them back to the front of the cabin. Carlos was nowhere to be seen. "Ike's out chopping trees. Well, tree. There's only one fallen tree left. And all we have is one axe. One very dull axe. It's really hard going. Be nice to have a saw, we could cut it up for firewood. Probably take all of us to drag it here as is. Maybe we can start on that addition, loghouse style, I guess."

"One more thing," Biscuit stopped LJ before they headed inside. "You saw the well, right?" LJ nodded. "Okay, the outhouse is down there," he pointed along a path. "Use it. Yeah?" LJ just nodded.

"Never shit upstream." Biscuit made sure he understood what he was telling him. "Ask Martha."

The cabin was about fifteen feet by twenty feet. Large enough for an open concept living room slash kitchen area, and two separate bedrooms. The kitchen had a cupboard and two drawers, each containing various bits and pieces; a fridge, powered by a propane tank long empty; and a sink, beside which, on a makeshift counter, lay a five-gallon jug. There was a couch, a table, and an upholstered chair in the living room, along with the treasured woodstove. Bunk beds in one of the bedrooms could sleep two; a double bed in the other could sleep another two. Which meant that LJ slept on the floor. He fell asleep wondering how hard it would be to haul a mattress from the dump. Should he find one. But no, he wouldn't. Or if he did, it would be completely disintegrated. The best he'd find is rusted box springs. And that wouldn't do. Maybe he could build an indoor double-sized sandbox. No, it would be impossible to haul that much sand from the beach …

Next day, LJ, Krush, Biscuit, and Tim spent the afternoon carrying huge chunks of wood, the result of Ike's labour, from the bush to the cabin.

"So, what's the story with Ike," LJ asked. "He used to be some kind of history teacher?"

"No," Tim replied, "he used to be some kind of head honcho in business."

"So how'd he get here?"

"'Profits in excess' and 'fraudulent advertising.'"

"What's that?"

"Theft over and lyin'," Biscuit grinned.

They continued heaving and grunting for a bit.

"Any idea when it starts getting cold?" LJ asked.

"No, but it'll be too soon whenever it is," Krush stood, stretched, and surveyed the area. "We ain't got near enough wood to last a winter."

"All I've got is this t-shirt," LJ noted.

"Yeah, me too," Tim said.

"There's a heavy coat in the cabin," Krush said. "Ed says we'll wear it whenever we go outside. One at a time," he added.

"I had a coat when I came here," Biscuit offered, "but it's long gone."

"They take your shoes too?"

"No," he replied. "Good thing too. It was winter. I would've lost my toes. And I love my toes."

They all stared at him.

"But not as much as I love my Daffy Duck watch."

After a while, LJ had another question. "So what happens to the guy who went nuts yesterday?"

"Carlos? He gets kicked out," Biscuit said.

"He gets exiled?"

As one, they burst out laughing.

The following morning, Tim and LJ tried to catch another rabbit to add to their collection. They didn't succeed. Not even close.

That afternoon, LJ had the idea of building a trap. It took the rest of the day. And it didn't work.

It took all of the next day. And it still didn't work.

The problem was there wasn't any more chicken wire—the cages they were using had been at the cabin when they'd found it—so he was using twigs, trying to weave them into panels. Initially, the twigs kept breaking when he wove them. So then he looked for different twigs. But they still broke. So then he looked for greener twigs. That worked. He ended up with two woven pieces, each about one square foot, but since the twigs were of different lengths, and he had nothing to cut them with, the ends stuck out rather messily.

After three days' work, he had six squares, but then he realized he didn't know how to fasten them together into a box.

So he went in search of grass, weeds, reeds—something. It took a whole day to find something that worked. He painstakingly hinged the front piece, the door, so it swung in and out. He propped the door open, open inward, with a stick, and when he knocked the stick over, poking it from the outside with a longer stick, the door closed. He was delighted. But then he realized the door swung out as easily as it swung in, so the rabbit could just walk out.

He added a lip to the bottom of the front piece. Again he propped the door open with a stick, and again when he knocked the stick over, the door closed. But because of the lip, it couldn't swing out. The rabbit would be trapped inside. He went in search of Tim.

"Hey, Tim!" he called excitedly. "Come check this out!"

LJ demonstrated his rabbit cage trap to Tim. Tim was excited at first, but then he stared at it a bit, and became less excited.

"No, that won't work," he said finally. He went into the cabin and came back out with the cabin's only towel. "Watch." He held the door wide open, then put the bunched up towel inside. When he let the door fall, it just fell down on top of the towel. "The door will come down on top of the rabbit, and it'll probably just jerk away, back out of the cage."

"Shit!" LJ shouted angrily. Then quickly tried to calm down before he drew the attention of Ed or John. But he'd spent a week on the thing! How could he have been so stupid?

"You just need to make it longer," Tim said. "So the rabbit is way at the back when the door closes, yeah?"

"Yeah." But he was tired. And overcome with inertia.

But by their next week at the cabin, he was refreshed enough to try again. The work went more quickly, now that he knew what twigs to look for. Still it took all day to find enough of them.

Next day, he started weaving four new, longer sides. At one point, he became really frustrated—too many twigs started breaking. Just before he smashed the whole thing, he got up and walked away, remembering Ed's advice, and warning. He didn't know that John and Anthony were taking turns watching him.

When he returned to his task, he realized that he could use the front and back of the earlier version. He just needed to replace the four sides. By mid-afternoon, he finished the fourth side. He tied them all together again, added the lip, rigged the door, and tried the trap. He called Tim again, with reservation.

Tim came around from the garden.

"Ready for a test drive again," LJ said. With cautious hope.

Tim went inside for the towel, then tested the trap, though he saw at a glance that it would work.

"Yeah, man, you've got it!" He high-fived him. LJ was happy. LJ was, yes, proud. For perhaps the first time in his life.

"What are we gonna use for bait though?" Tim asked.

LJ looked blankly at Tim. He hadn't thought that far ahead. "I dunno. We got no carrots." It was just a setback, he told himself. It didn't mean that the whole thing had been a complete fucking waste of time. "What do you feed your rabbits? What do they like?"

"Well what I feed them, and what they like, is pretty much everywhere. So why would they go into the cage for some?"

"Right." LJ struggled with the possibility that it *had* been a complete— "Okay, we—how about an apple?" They'd picked some on their way from the beach. "They wouldn't find those all over the place. And they might like it. It's crunchy. Like carrots. Rabbits like carrots, right?"

"It's worth a try. Only we leave tomorrow."

"Can't we ask one of the others to try it out?"

Tim thought a minute. "Yeah. Juan. He'll do it."

At about noon the next day, Henry, Tapper, Juan, and Ike arrived. LJ showed Juan his new rabbit trap. Everyone watched his demonstration, then cheered. LJ felt good. Very good. Juan enthusiastically agreed to find a good spot for it, bait it, and check it every day.

"In the meantime," he said, "we should build a larger cage."

"Or an enclosure of some sort," Ike suggested. "We don't need the top, do we?"

"Rabbits can hop, Ike."

"Yeah, but can they jump? And if so, how high?"

The beach group left them to their ruminations, confident they'd figure it out.

11

That night at the beach, when they were sitting around the fire, LJ said, "So I was thinking—"

Biscuit blurted out a laugh. LJ grinned. Both John and Anthony smiled. It wasn't long ago that LJ would've stomped off in anger.

"I'm going to the window tomorrow," he continued.

"Your Mr. Morgan is meeting you there again?" Anthony asked.

"Well, maybe. It's been a while—and we didn't exactly—but if he is, if he's there, I was thinking we could ask him for stuff."

"But he can't give us anything," Tim said.

"Not real—not physical stuff, I get that. But he can give us information, can't he? And we need that, right?"

The men were suddenly very interested.

"Ask him how to make matches," Krush said. "And shoes," he added, nodding at John's feet. "Ask him how to make shoes."

"And a CD player," Tim suggested, looking at Anthony.

"And a TV," Biscuit said happily. "Make a list," he added, "write that down."

They all turned to look at him, and he continued without missing a beat, "Ask him how to make paper. And a pen."

"And indoor plumbing," Tim said.

"And a fridge!" Biscuit added.

"Why don't you just ask him how to make circuit boards," John interjected angrily. "That way we could build a computer and get all this information on our own.

Hey, I know! We could build a satellite dish. Ask him how to build a satellite dish. Write that down."

The men were silent for a bit.

"Okay, what about electricity," Tim persisted, in a small voice. "What's his name invented that back in the dark ages. Can't be too difficult."

John sighed. As did Ed.

"We don't have the stuff we'd need to make any of that even if we did know how," Anthony explained. "We'd need PVC pipes for plumbing. And copper wire for electricity. Where are we going to get copper?"

"Maybe the mineralogy department of Princeton could come to the window and give us a lecture," John said sarcastically. "Hell, it shouldn't take them too long to explain everything we need to know about copper mining." The young ones had no idea. No idea what they lost when they were exiled.

"Maybe we can ask only about stuff we can follow up on," Anthony suggested gently.

The men were silent again.

"Ask him how to make soap," Anthony said. "We've got ash and eventually we'll have animal fat. I think—"

"We don't need soap," John said dismissively. "Aren't we doing okay with sand, and swimming in the lake?"

There was a silence. They all look pointedly at John.

Biscuit turned back to LJ. "Ask him how to make soap. Write that down. In the sand," he added.

That broke the tension a bit.

"Do we need something special for matches?" Tim asked. He honestly didn't know.

"Sulfur," Anthony said.

"Okay, what about candles? Could we make candles?"

"Maybe," he replied, "especially if we can make soap." He nodded to LJ to add that to the list. In his head.

"What we need is information about how to live off

the land," Ed said. "There must be plants out there that we could use in a hundred ways. Just knowing what to eat and what not to eat—we're lucky we haven't poisoned ourselves yet."

"And there must be a way to make some sort of shelter without bricks and plywood and stuff," Krush suggested, "maybe even without logs, since trees are so frickin' hard to carry." He rolled his shoulders. Every time he spent a day hauling chunks of wood, he was stiff the next morning.

"So that's what you want me to ask him?" LJ confirmed, but confused about what exactly he was confirming, since so much had been suggested.

"He could just look it all up on his smartphone," Tim suggested.

"I don't know if he has one," LJ said. "He's pretty old."

"Might not work out here anyway," John grimaced. "We don't know where the nearest cell tower is."

"But he could get a survival handbook from the library," Ed suggested, "and read it to us."

"Old school!" Biscuit said, then laughed.

"But how are we going to remember a whole book?" Tim asked.

"We'll have to get everyone there," John was coming around to the idea. "Each of us can remember something."

"I can make little songs out of the words for everyone," Anthony suggested. "Be easier to remember that way."

"Who said the humanities are useless?" Ed noted dryly, then smiled at Anthony.

There was a pause in the conversation, but it was a good pause. Instead of the usual mix of dejection, boredom, anger, and fatigue, there was an energy, a hope, among the members of the group.

"But how are we going to pay him?" LJ asked. "I mean, we can't, we shouldn't just take it for free, right?

“Yeah,” John fell back into despair, not even noticing the importance of LJ’s asking the question. “It’s not like we can just hand him some money or whatever.”

“Wait a minute,” Anthony said, thinking. “Does your Mr. Morgan like music?”

“I don’t know, why?”

“We can give him a concert! That should be worth, what, twenty bucks?”

“Say what?” Biscuit asked in mock horror. “Baby, we are so fine!” He turned to LJ. “Tell the man we’ve got a hundred-dollar concert for him!”

12

It was raining the next day, and it was cold, which made for an unpleasant walk, but LJ had committed himself... The others let themselves be assured that he'd be okay by himself. After all, he'd come back the first time. And it was raining, and cold ...

They had a sort of canopy on four poles they put over the fire on days like this, which worked pretty well, but they did need to tend the fire more vigilantly. Otherwise, on days like this, they just huddled in their tent, such as it was, and their lean-to ...

"Hello? Mr. Morgan? Are you there?" He had no idea, really, what time it was. But since he had no idea what time it had been before ...

"Yes, I'm here. Is that you, LJ?"

"Yeah! How're you doin'?"

"I'm doing fine, thank you. And yourself?"

"Oh, well ... I'm glad you came back." He was. He just realized that. And not just because of his mission.

"Well, that's good. It's a long drive. I wasn't actually sure you'd be here. You weren't here last week."

"No, we—I was somewhere else and—sorry about that." The man had driven a long way for nothing. And yet, he had come yet again?

"But I thought I'd try once more. Wasn't sure I would, though, to be honest—"

"Well you did, and I'm glad. I have a—a proposition to make."

"Oh? What kind of a proposition?" he asked, curious, and a bit concerned. "I can't help you get out, you know."

"I know. I'm not asking for that."

"Okay …"

"I'm asking—I'd like to ask—for information. We need to know stuff. There's a bunch of guys in here, and they're—we're—I'm part of them now. They're good guys," he hastened to add, for some reason. "I haven't fallen in with the wrong crowd, we're trying to—" LJ was exasperated with his incoherence. But so much had happened to him, so much had changed, *he* had changed…

"We don't know stuff," he tried again. "And we thought maybe you could tell us stuff. We thought maybe you could give us information. But not for free," he rushed on. "I mean, we'd pay you. We're not asking for a handout."

"I see." Mr. Morgan was pleased. Especially about that last part. "And how are you going to pay me?" he asked, supportive of the idea, not challenging it.

"Do you like music?"

"Yes, as a matter of fact, I do."

"Well, we'd like to give you a concert. There's a group here, they're called Rapap—" he stumbled over the word. "Rap-a-capella." John had broken it down for him. "They're really somethin' too, you should hear them. I mean even if you don't agree to this."

"All right, I would like to hear them. But I'll have to think about the other. I'm not sure it's—let me think about it."

"Okay. Good. Thanks. If you come back next week—actually, can you make it two weeks? We're at the cabin in between. If you do agree, well, what we were thinking we need most is information about how to live off the land. What to eat, what not to eat, how to build a shelter without, you know, saws and nails and all the stuff we don't have. Oh, and soap. We'd like to know how to make soap.

And candles."

"You need a survival guide."

"Yeah!" That's what Ed had called it.

"Well, okay, let me think about it, and maybe look around."

"Okay, great. Thanks. Thank you."

LJ left. Mr. Morgan stayed for a bit, staring at the wall, once again trying to see the other side.

Back home, he carried his after-dinner cup of coffee into the living room. It was a modest but comfortable room. Retro, his daughter would call it. CDs, stereo, books, and some knick knacks filled the shelves on the wall to the left of the large window, and a TV was set into the wall on the right. He turned on a reading light by his recliner chair, set his coffee onto the side table, beside the weekend issue of the newspaper, then lowered himself into his favourite chair with a sigh. He turned on the TV with the remote.

Janet, his wife, entered the room as well, also carrying a cup of coffee and some healthy snacks. She set her coffee and the snacks on the coffee table and stretched out on the couch.

"We should've sent out for a pizza," Mr. Morgan said. The salad they'd had was nutritious enough, but not filling. And he *liked* pizza.

"We should be in our twenties again," she smiled ruefully.

"That would be nice," he agreed, and gave her a wink.

"So," he opened the conversation a few moments later, "LJ made a proposition to me today."

"LJ is in no position to be making propositions to anyone." It was a bit harsh, but wasn't she right?

"Well, that may be. Still. He asked if I could bring him

some information."

"Information?"

"Well, it seems there's a group of them in there, out there, trying to make a go of it, and, well, they don't know much."

"And whose fault is that?"

He glanced over at her. "Do *you* know how to make soap?"

"How to make what?"

"That's one of the things they want to know. How to make soap. Could you do that?" He gestured to the room then. "Could you make a CD player? A cup? We wouldn't be any better off. They've got nothing, Janet. Think about it. No electricity, no plumbing. No tools. Not to mention books, television, computers. The fruits of centuries of civilization." He picked up a bottle of aspirin from the side table, and took one. "Aspirin, for god's sake. How are those boys ever going to invent aspirin?"

"They're not boys. And they should have thought of that before they turned their back on society, on the fruits of centuries of civilization." She turned down the TV with their second remote control and faced him.

"Someone spent seven or eight years going to classes," she said, "studying chemistry, biology, what have you, and then probably another five years experimenting, trying this and that, before they finally came up with aspirin. And then someone had to put together a company to make it. And distribute it. All so we can buy a hundred of them for a mere three dollars. Which is not *nearly* enough, not nearly what it's worth. To you, to me—

"Speaking of which," she reached out her hand, "Give me one of those." She took an aspirin with a swallow of coffee, then massaged her temples a bit. "I swear those kids are getting worse every day. One of the grade nines called me a bitch today because we had only pudding for dessert. He wanted jello."

Mr. Morgan grinned. Though it wasn't really funny. Her job at the school cafeteria wasn't easy, given kids today. She had to take a lot of abuse.

"Same with electricity, plumbing, television, books," she continued after a moment. "Someone, lots of someones, put a lot of work into all those things. And your LJ should have thought of all that before he said 'Fuck you!' Not once, not twice, but three times."

Mr. Morgan agreed, and yet— "Surely they still have rights. They're still human!"

"Are you talking about human rights? Are you saying that just because you're human, you're entitled to certain things? No siree, I don't agree with you there. Takes more than that. You have to *earn* rights. You want the right to borrow books from the library? You have to agree to take care of them and return them on time. You want the right to drive a car? You have to learn how to drive one, get a license, buy insurance, and agree to follow the rules of the road. And even if we do have rights just 'because', surely those rights can be forfeited. You return those books all torn up, or you don't return them at all, you lose the right to borrow more."

"Yes, but food, shelter—"

"You *pay* for it. *We* pay for it. We pay for the fruits of other people's labor. How long have you been collecting garbage to do just that? And why do you think I've been working at that damn cafeteria all these years? I *swear* those kids are getting worse," she said again, massaging her temples again before continuing. "We have a right to it because we pay for it. Why should they get a free ride? Are they disabled in some way? Are they children? Are they elderly?"

"You're right," he conceded. Hadn't he said as much to LJ that first time? "But it's supposed to be exile, not punishment. And if all we're saying is 'Hey, make your own society,' well that's exactly what they're trying to do. And isn't trade between societies acceptable?"

In theory, she supposed, what he was saying made sense, but in practice— "What have they got to trade?"

"Well," he replied sheepishly, "they say they're going to give me a concert."

She snorted. "And in return, you'd what, read to them from some survival book."

"That's the plan, yes."

She looked over at him warmly. He had a good heart— "Okay, but why you? You don't owe this LJ anything."

"Don't I? I keep feeling that if I'd said something to him— I saw that boy twice a week for all of his twenty-three years."

"He had a father. And a mother. And teachers. And rehab. I'm sure someone did say something to him. More than once. More than twice. He just wasn't prepared to listen."

"Well, he's prepared now."

"Well it's a little too late now." She heard herself. When had she become so hard?

"Do you even know if it'd be legal?" She changed direction. "How'd you find out about this window anyway?"

"Fellow at work. His younger brother was exiled. He visited him at this window a couple of times, but then the kid just stopped showing up. Feared the worst, of course."

She nodded, understanding. The both turned back to the TV for a while, but they'd come back to this. They'd figure it out. Or at least he would. It was his call, his choice.

13

It was switch day. As they approached the cabin, LJ immediately saw his rabbit cage trap by the door, completely in pieces. He rushed toward the door, hollering for Juan. Tim and Krush were right behind him.

Juan came out of the cabin, and LJ gave him a shove. "What gives you the right—" Tim and Krush grabbed him before he could give Juan another shove.

"Took me a whole week to make that!" LJ protested, shrugging them off.

"Hey!" Ed stood inches from LJ's face, daring him to lose it and take a swing at him. Tim and Krush hustled him away, one on each side, Biscuit covering the rear.

"And here just past the palatial ballroom," he said in a bored British accent, "next to the multi-media entertainment center, we have the time-out room."

"I didn't do it, man," Juan called out to LJ. "Why would I? Think! I set it like you said, and when I went out to check it the next day, it was all bust up."

"So someone else found it," Tim suggested. "Took the rabbit and broke the trap to bits." Suddenly he raced around to the back of the cabin.

"But why?" LJ wailed, still angry. "That doesn't make any sense! Why not just take the rabbit? Or the whole trap? I spent a whole fucking week making that thing!"

Ed spoke under his breath to John. "Oh my. A whole week. Friend of mine had his dissertation wiped out by some stupid kid's email virus. Three years he'd spent on the thing."

"Maybe we should cut him some slack," John said.

"Probably never spent a whole week working on anything before."

"You're probably right," Ed sighed. "Still."

LJ continued to huff and puff.

"He didn't keep a back-up?" John asked calmly, his eyes on LJ.

"He did," Ed replied, his eyes also on LJ. "Never checked it. Turns out the disk was defective."

"That sucks."

"That's life."

Two hours later, LJ was making another rabbit trap. Tim's two rabbits had been taken as well. And the grouse. Fortunately, the chicken wire had just been sort of crumpled, so Tim was able to repair the pen. Anthony was trying to expand their garden. Krush, Ed, and John were wrestling with another chunk of Ike's felled tree. Biscuit and Tim were further out, collecting kindling and looking for berries. Or something besides apples.

"Could've been a fox," Tim said to Biscuit, as they walked deeper into the bush.

"What?"

"Whoever wrecked LJ's trap. And my cage. Maybe it was a fox."

"Still would've been intentional," Biscuit grinned, "and definitely a crime."

Tim agreed, then started wondering how a fox normally caught a rabbit, whether it was just a matter of its superior speed, or whether a pack coordinated their efforts, and whether that was accidental cooperation or something more strategic—when suddenly they heard a helicopter.

"What the fuck?!" Biscuit looked up.

They started to run up the next rise, toward where it

seemed to be planning to land. As they got to the top of the hill, they saw several men already at the spot. Tim wanted to keep going, to get up close, but Biscuit held him back.

"Wait a minute. Think. They're sure as hell not comin' for us. And there might be trouble. So we may as well stay here."

"But—"

"Sssh—" Biscuit strained to hear what the men were saying. Impossible until the helicopter landed and the motor was turned off.

No one got out.

Some of the men walked closer to it.

Suddenly a loud and clear command was issued from inside, over a speaker. "Please stay back from the helicopter. I repeat, please move away from the helicopter."

"Sounds like the guy from those old ING commercials," Tim noted.

"'Save your money,'" Biscuit did a good imitation, then giggled. At the thought of having money to save.

When the men obeyed, and stepped back, someone got out of the helicopter. He was uniformed and holding a gun. A big gun. Another man, or guard, crouched in the doorway. Also armed.

"Thank you," the first one said. "Is there a Dr. Arnold Morrison here?"

The gathered men looked at each other. Then one of them stepped forward.

"Please stay back from the helicopter!"

The man stepped back. Then shouted to be heard. "Yeah. He's not here now, but I've seen him around. Newcomer, right?"

"Tell him we will be back in one half hour. He must be here in one half hour, yes?"

"Take me at least that long to find him," the man protested.

The guard glanced back, but kept his gun aimed at the crowd. The crouched one turned and conferred with the occupants of the helicopter, then turned back and said something to the standing guard.

"One hour. We will be back in one hour."

The helicopter took off. The man who had spoken looked around for a moment in surprise, and indecision, then headed off at a run.

"Anthony! John!" Tim called out as soon as they were close enough to the cabin to be heard.

"Hey, anyone here?" Biscuit shouted, joining him. They'd run back the whole way.

Anthony rushed from around the back, relief splashing across his face when he saw that Tim was okay. LJ and Krush followed. Ed and John hurried out from inside. None of them ever 'cried wolf', so—

"There was a helicopter!" Tim said. "It landed and two guys came out asking for a Dr. Morrison."

"A helicopter? Landed here in exile? Are you sure?"

Tim gave him a look.

"Of course you are," Anthony said. "Sorry."

"Well isn't that a precedent," Ed commented, scratching his chin.

"Who's Dr. Morrison?" John asked. "Anyone know?"

"Actually, yeah," Ed said. "I heard from one of the others about two new guys. One's a governor. Ex-governor. He was caught rigging his election. He'd already been caught accepting illegal political contributions and awarding contracts to his friends. The other one was a physician. Out for performing abortions. Or euthanasia. One of the sanctity of life crimes. So-called crimes."

"So who were the guys in the helicopter? Were they Americans?" John looked at Tim and Biscuit. That wouldn't make sense.

"I don't think so," Tim said. "The one who spoke had an accent. Like the ING guy."

"Maybe Denmark is willing to accept Dr. Morrison into their society," Ed suggested. A Danish accent and a Dutch accent would probably sound the same to them. "Well, well, it does happen." He'd heard of it, but hadn't really believed it.

"If they find him," Tim said. "They said they'd be back in an hour. We gotta find this Dr. Morrison and let him know!"

"Hang on," Anthony reached out. "Why do *you* have to find him? You don't even know him."

Tim ignored him, turning to Ed. "Do you know where he is?"

"Sorry," Ed shook his head.

"Well, I'm going back anyway," Biscuit said, and Tim nodded his agreement. "See what happens. Anyone coming?

"Hell, yeah," John said. "I'm curious too."

"Me too," Krush said.

They all wanted to go. Nothing like this had ever happened before. But they couldn't leave the cabin unattended. Ed offered to stay, as did Anthony and LJ. And, as an afterthought, Krush. If whoever had trashed LJ's trap thought about coming back for more, now, when everyone was thought to be somewhere else, would be a good time.

"Keep your distance!" Anthony yelled at Tim. "John–?"

"Yeah." He understood.

So Biscuit, Tim, and John headed off. Anthony returned to the back of the cabin, Ed and Krush went back to the chunk of tree they'd been struggling with, and LJ went back to his rabbit trap.

The three of them lay on the hill, at a safe distance. Quite a crowd had formed, and even from where they were, they could feel the picnic atmosphere.

"Why wouldn't they come for us?" Tim said to Biscuit, responding to what he'd said earlier. "I mean, I ain't so bad, am I?"

"If you were a society," Biscuit said, "would you welcome someone who just took stuff all the time without paying?"

"Maybe."

Biscuit looked at him as if to say 'Yeah, right.'

"Maybe if I'd had the money, I would've paid for it," Tim protested.

"And why didn't you have the money?"

"Because I didn't have a job."

"And why didn't you have a job?"

"Because I couldn't find one."

"Double-D Burger's always hiring," Biscuit said, after a moment.

"Yeah," Tim admitted. "But at what they pay, take me forever to get what I want."

"And I want it NOWWWW!!" Biscuit wailed, like a baby.

Tim laughed.

"What was it *you* wanted so bad?" he asked Biscuit a moment later.

"You know, I don't even remember," he replied, uncharacteristically sober. And clearly disgusted with himself.

"Couldn't've been that important to you."

Biscuit's silence was agreement.

"There's a lot of guys collecting unemployment," Tim said then, "and what do you call it, 'benefits.' 'Oh my back hurts.' Why don't *they* get a job at Double-D?"

A little while later, they heard the helicopter approach and saw it land. John wondered then why stuff couldn't be dropped off. Into exile. By whoever. No, the forcefield would have to be deactivated, as it surely had been for this. Damn, he should've sent someone to the wall to test that. *He* should've gone to the wall to test that. No, he mentally reprimanded himself for being so stupid, so desperate—surely they could deactivate individual sectors. Like the one the helicopter had entered through.

"Please stay back!" The command interrupted his thoughts. No one had come out of the helicopter yet. They were using the comm system, which was apparently hooked up to a loudspeaker. "Do not approach the helicopter without permission."

"Sounds like the ING guy, right?" Tim asked John.

"It does."

"If you do, you will be shot," the voice continued. "We do not want to do this, but we will do this. Is Dr. Arnold Morrison here?"

No one said anything. No one stepped forward. Then someone pointed. And everyone turned to see a man in the distance, running. Trying to run. He had his hand raised slightly. He was badly out of breath and almost staggering.

"I think that's him," one of the men near the helicopter said.

"Duh. Ya think?" Biscuit couldn't resist. John and Tim grinned.

The door opened, and one of the uniformed guards jumped to the ground, carefully keeping his gun at the ready. Again, a second guard crouched in the doorway, keeping his eyes on the crowd.

Everyone waited in silence as the man got closer.

When he was close enough to be heard, he rasped out, "I am Dr. Arnold Morrison." He fell to his knees, gulping oxygen. Obviously not one of those over-achieving doctors who run marathons in their spare time. And he wasn't young. But he'd known, no doubt, that he was running for his life.

"Please step forward and show your ID at the window."

"Oh no," John groaned.

One of the men stepped forward as if to help the doctor to his feet.

"Step away!" the guard on the ground warned.

The man stepped back, raising his hands.

Dr. Morrison got to his feet, unassisted, then pulled a wallet out of his back pocket.

"Seriously?" John muttered. And wondered what door he'd been delivered to.

He stumbled toward the helicopter and held it up at the window. The window slid open and a hand took the ID. After a moment's conference, the disembodied voice spoke again.

"Dr. Morrison only, please." The first guard took stepped forward, as if to 'cover' him. "Everyone else, please do not approach the helicopter. I repeat that we will shoot."

As the other guard reached down to help Dr. Morrison up and into the helicopter, one of the men in the crowd shouted out, "If you take him, you take me too! We all want out of here!" He started walking confidently toward the helicopter door.

And the first guard shot him. Just like that.

Dr. Morrison hesitated, horrified. He must have reconsidered, for just a second, but then he continued, quickly, to get inside.

They watched the helicopter take off. And then they continued to watch it, until it was—gone.

14

A few weeks later, the beach group was gathered at the window. This was the day. This was the time. Biscuit consulted his Daffy Duck watch. Again. Everyone in the group was excited. For knowledge. Who'd've thought?

"Hello? Mr. Morgan?" LJ called out.

"LJ?"

"Yeah! Yes! You came!" He wouldn't've blamed him if he didn't. At least, not as much as he would've—was it just a couple months ago?

"I did."

"And—"

"And I have a book with me—"

The men cheered.

He'd also brought a lawn chair the group would groan to see, which he set up near the window. His car was parked nearby. Of course they'd groan even louder to see that.

"I don't know how much of it will be useful to you," he called out, "but— I'll guess we'll see."

"Thank you, Mr. Morgan," Anthony spoke up. "I'm Anthony. And there's Tim here, and Krush, and Biscuit—we're Rapacapella. And Ed and John, they're here too."

"All right." He felt a little blind, unable to see any of them.

"We thought we'd give you your concert first," Anthony continued, "because once you start reading, we're going to have to concentrate on remembering what you read. Is that okay with you?"

"Yes, that's fine." He settled comfortably into his chair.

"All right. This first song, you might know it, it's called 'In the Still of the Night.'"

They started singing a rap-acapella version of the song. Mr. Morgan smiled. It had been one of his wedding songs.

When they'd finished, that song and half a dozen others they'd practiced, Mr. Morgan applauded. "That was truly exceptional. I thank you, gentlemen. Really. It's a shame—" he stopped in mid-sentence. But they all knew what he was going to say.

"Well," he continued, a little awkwardly, "I guess I'd better be starting my end of the deal. I've marked several spots—I think you'll like this first one. Dandelion coffee."

"Coffee!!" Biscuit shouted. "Gimme that one!" he turned to Anthony.

"It says here that you take dandelion roots," Mr. Morgan read, "you all know what a dandelion looks like, I imagine, well you wash and scrape the roots. Then you dry them by a fire until they're black. Don't let them touch the flames though. Then you cut them up and grind them. I guess it'll end up like coffee grounds. Then, well, it says you use one teaspoon per cup."

"Okay," Anthony said, "Mr. Morgan, if you could just wait a minute—I'm going to turn each bit of information into a little song, so it's easier to remember. Hang on—" He thought for a bit, then turned to Biscuit and sang, to the tune of 'I'm a Little Teapot':

"Dandelion roots get washed and scraped,
"Then you let them dry by the fire till black.
"Then you cut them up and grind them good,
"Here you go, your coffee, Mac!"

Biscuit wandered off to the side and started singing his 'I'm a Little Teapot—Dandelion Coffee' song. As soon as he did the handle and spout gestures, Anthony, Tim, and

Krush started laughing. When he added movements for washing, scraping, and cutting, LJ and John broke into smiles. At 'grind them good', Biscuit swung his hips in a circle like he had a hula hoop, an extra large hula hoop, and even Ed relaxed. The group, previously daunted by the task ahead, lightened.

"Okay, we're ready for the next bit," Anthony said, once he'd confirmed that Biscuit had the words right.

"All right," Mr. Morgan replied. "Now I didn't find a soap recipe I thought you could use, but there's a plant called soapwort that can be found in sunny fields. Apparently you can boil a handful of leaves or roots in a pint of water and get a lathery liquid."

"And does the book describe it? Is there a picture?" Anthony asked, then turned to the group. "Anyone know what soapwort looks like?"

All of them shook their heads.

"Well, it says it has a single flower," Mr. Morgan said, "with five pink petals, and the leaves are green, shiny, and spear-shaped."

Anthony concentrated, humming fragments that went nowhere. "I'm having trouble with this one..." he muttered, frustrated, no doubt feeling the pressure.

"I'll take it," Ed said. "I've got a ton of case law in my head, one's Soap vs. Regina, if you can believe it. May as well get some use out of it. I'll just add a couple notwithstanding clauses..." He stepped toward the window and said loudly enough for Mr. Morgan to hear: "Notwithstanding a single flower exhibiting five pink petals and shiny, green, spear-shaped leaves, the defendant did on the night in question boil a handful of leaves or roots in a pint of water."

"You've got it," Mr. Morgan smiled.

"Gotta find another pot," John muttered, and planned a trip to the dump.

"Okay, this next one…" The process continued with Mr. Morgan reading a bit, Anthony turning it into something memorable, then presenting it to the next waiting man.

By mid-afternoon, each member of the group had been assigned several songs, so they were glad—relieved is more like it—when, by prior arrangement, the cabin group showed up.

"Now, the rest of what I have marked," Mr. Morgan said, after Ike, Tapper, Henry, and Juan had each taken a bit, "is just miscellaneous, I guess. Stuff that's good for you to know, I think. For example, dandelion juice is apparently rich in minerals and vitamins. And spruce needles—they should be fresh, green—have a lot of vitamin C. You can either chew on the needles or make a tea. And then there's a list of stuff that's poisonous—"

"Hang on," Anthony said, "give me a minute."

Dick was next in line. He was a newcomer, recently accepted into the cabin group.

"I'm all out of songs, so try this one as a nursery rhyme." He proceeded to recite in a singsong voice:

"Dandelions, dandelions, all I see,
"Minerals and vitamins, good for me.
"Fresh green spruce, needles and tea,
"Got to get my vitamin C."

Dick just nodded and wandered away from the group.

"Wait a minute," Anthony said. "Stay here and say it to yourself. A few times to be sure you've got it."

"I ain't no school kid," Dick retorted. "This is shit."

"Hey!" Tim said harshly to him. "Do it! He knows what he's doing. Taught me a lot of stuff." He looked at Anthony then. "Only reason I didn't learn half of it was my own damn fault."

Anthony nodded, accepting the praise and the apology.

"That's your problem," Dick said.

"Yours too, man," LJ tried.

But Dick kept walking. Away.

"You can lead a horse to water," John said.

"But you can't make it think," Tapper finished.

"Well, that's about it," Mr. Morgan said an hour or so later. "The rest of what's in here doesn't seem to apply to this part of the country."

"We're about full anyway," Ed spoke up. He and Anthony had taken most of the last half hour of material, as revised case law and rewritten arias, respectively. "And we'd like to get back before dark."

"Thank you, Mr. Morgan," Anthony said.

"Yeah, thanks. A lot," LJ said.

The others also expressed their thanks, individually and with some ceremony.

"Oh you're quite welcome," Mr. Morgan said. "And thank you once again for the concert. I'll leave you then," he stood and started to fold up his lawn chair. "I confess I'm a bit eager to get back—the 400 is on tonight—" Again, he stopped in mid-sentence.

"The Olympics!" Tim cried out, suddenly realizing what Mr. Morgan was talking about. "We're missing the Olympics!"

"Shit!" LJ was equally upset. "I'm gonna miss my man Jaheel do the hundred in under 9!"

"Under 9? Man, no one's done it in under 9—"

"Yeah, but Jaheel, he's gonna do it this year, I can feel it. Say Mr. Morgan, when the hundred is on, could you record—"

There was a sudden, awkward silence all round. A sudden, overwhelming sadness all round.

"Good-bye, Mr. Morgan," John said, for all of them. "And thanks again."

15

The days passed. They all had their first cup of dandelion coffee. Not nearly as good as Doritos, Biscuit pronounced. Spruce tea became part of their evening sit-around-the-fire. They hadn't yet found any soapwort, or clover, or chickweed, or prairie turnips, or any of the other edibles Mr. Morgan had told them about, but they kept looking.

In addition to those scouting missions, a pair of them went almost every day to the dump. It had occurred to John that the dump might have started as a pit, possibly covered with a layer of dirt every now and then to help the decomposition process. So, he said, they should become 'trash archaeologists'—they needed to not just pick through the crap they could see, but to dig. Like LJ had done, but much deeper. Digging for buried treasures, Biscuit said. And indeed, a good-sized stainless steel pot was found on their fourth dig. Handle intact.

"Hey LJ," Tapper called out when the beach group arrived on the next switch day, "We discovered what bait will attract your rabbits!"

"Yeah?" he was excited. "What?"

"My garden!"

He led the group around to the back.

"Wow," John said. The entire garden was enclosed with panels like those on LJ's rabbit cage trap. "That must be twenty cages worth!"

"Twenty-one. Juan calculated." He grinned.

"But look at the sprouts!" Ed said, as if everyone was

missing the really important thing. Which they were. A dozen green sprouts, of something or other, had pushed up through the earth.

Tapper beamed proudly.

"Dusk and dawn is when the rabbits come," he explained then. "One of us has been on patrol since the sprouts appeared. Three days ago."

"We need a pellet gun," Tim suggested.

"Or a slingshot." That was Biscuit.

"Let's add elastics to our trashology list," John said.

In the meantime, Tapper explained, they'd tried throwing stones. Not rocks. They wanted to stun the rabbits, so they could catch and keep them. But in being careful not to damage the sprouts—which is why they weren't using the fistful-of-stones approach—they hadn't managed to hit any of the rabbits. The men nodded their understanding. The cabin group had done a massive amount of work during their week; it was now the beach group's turn to figure out a way to build on it.

And figure it out they did. Turned out Krush, who went on rabbit patrol that first dusk, had a wicked fast arm. *And* a good eye. But he couldn't catch the rabbits he stunned. So he enlisted Tim, Biscuit, and LJ for the morning patrol.

Still, the rabbits eluded them. It was frustrating because Tapper was right: the garden *was* bait. One time half a dozen rabbits showed up. And they couldn't catch even one of them.

Mid-week, at dawn, Tim, Biscuit, and LJ—all enthusiastic and fast, but still mentally half asleep—collided head on. Krush exploded with laughter, it was such an impressive and unexpected crash. They couldn't've done a better Three Stooges moment if they'd tried. Tim, quickest to realize what had happened—the three of them had found themselves on the ground in a heap, as stunned as the rabbit that had gotten away—joined Krush with a surprisingly loud laugh. Biscuit and LJ quickly added sheepish giggles.

Ed grumbled because their laughter had awakened him, but John, already up, smiled broadly. It had been a long time since he'd heard such unrestrained laughter. Anthony, who had also been awakened, was delighted to discover the reason. He couldn't remember the last time he saw his brother having fun.

"Have you noticed a change?" John asked Ed. They were carrying wood from Ike's newest chopping site. "In us? I mean, everyone? Since we've been here."

Ed stared at him. Duh.

John caught the look and grinned. "No, I mean—we're more cooperative than we would be on the outside. Back home."

Ed didn't say anything.

"Sure, it's rational to *be* cooperative here, but it's rational to be cooperative on the outside too. And yet we—men—seldom are."

They grunted a bit as they heaved a large piece off the ground.

"Got it?" Ed asked, shifting the weight of the thing a bit.

"Yeah," John replied. "Go slow though, I can't see my feet."

They manoeuvred around the other chunks of wood toward the path that led back to the cabin.

"I think it's the absence of TV," John said. "I think it affects us, has affected us, more than we think. I mean, we start watching it as soon as we're what, five years old? Outside of work, that's all most people do. They come home, they have supper, then they sit in front of the TV until they go to bed." He paused for a moment, remembering, that he'd never again just come home, have supper, then watch TV.

"And every man on TV is— When I got Netflix, I started watching a British cop drama, and I also watched one that was set in Sweden, I think, and they were both really different from your standard Hollywood fare. The people, the men, they weren't so bloody obsessed with being one-up on the next guy.

"Here, men learn that that's all that matters. Every moment of every day, a man wonders if he's one-up or one-down. It sours relationships. Even meeting a girl is something to brag about to your buddies, a way to be one-up. It's not about the girl at all."

"Competition," Ed agreed. "Winning at all costs." He was thinking back to his law school days. "It's addictive."

"Our obsession with sports doesn't help," John observed. "I wonder if there's fifty channels of sports twenty-four-seven in Britain and Sweden."

"Don't forget to use your legs," Ed said as they carefully set the chunk onto the ground in front of the cabin. They couldn't afford a hernia or slipped disc.

"You know," John continued as he straightened, then stretched, "I think we're all in here for trying to 'be a man' one way or another. Have you ever read John Stoltenberg's stuff?"

Ed shook his head.

"I did, just before I came here. Wish I'd found it when I was fifteen."

That afternoon, John saw Tim, Biscuit, and LJ out front crouched in the dirt. At first, unlikely as it would be, he thought they might be playing marbles. But then he saw that they had a stick and were taking turns, sort of, drawing in the dirt.

"Whatcha' doin'?" he asked, approaching the threesome.

"We're making a Rabbit Playbook," Biscuit said. "See, this is the garden, and here's where Krush stands, hidden, and this is where LJ, Tim, and me are. Now if the rabbit is *here* when it's hit," he drew a pair of rabbit ears near one corner of the garden, "Tim will go left, like this," he drew a line in the dirt, "LJ will go right, here, and I'll sprint to here in case it makes it past them both. We're calling that play 'Bugs Bunny.'

"And," he smoothed the dirt, erasing the play, "if the rabbit's *here*," he drew a pair of rabbit ears in another corner, "it can only go this way, so I'll tackle it here, but if it slips out of my reach, Tim's gonna have me covered here. That's 'Roger Rabbit.'

"Wouldn't it be better," Tim took the stick from Biscuit, "if I went *here* ..."

John grinned, impressed, then left them to—'The Easter Bunny'?

The weeks passed. The Rabbit Playbook worked, and they managed to add several rabbits to their collection. Given what had happened with LJ's cage trap, they set up a round-the-clock guard of their enlarged rabbit cage and were delighted when a litter of five little bunnies appeared.

Tim managed to catch another grouse. And another. He built a nest of sorts inside the cage, and every day they checked, they hoped, for eggs.

They collected apples and berries and tried to figure out how to preserve them. They tried just leaving them in the sun, but they didn't end up with the dried fruit John used to buy at the bulk bins store. They ended up instead with rotten fruit. They tried making apple sauce and jam, and that seemed to work, but they ended up with only a dozen variously-sized containers of the stuff. They would have been able to make more, but when they went back to pick more apples, they discovered that every single apple on every single tree they knew about had been picked. Ripe and not. Many of them were on the ground, rotten beyond use. The beaters. How could they be so stupid? How could they not be as hungry as the rest of them? Krush, LJ, and Anthony spent two days planting the seeds, in a variety of places, and Tapper set aside a couple dozen to plant in spring.

They also experimented with the fish they caught. John suspected they needed salt to preserve it properly, but they didn't know where to find salt.

Although they continued to struggle with the plan of adding an addition to the cabin, it wasn't succeeding, even with the scrap sheets of aluminum they'd started unearthing. So they accepted Ed's idea about living underground, and started digging in earnest, taking turns with the good shovel and the hard-soled but without-laces construction boots they'd found. The days were getting a little shorter. And a little colder.

But they were dismayed to find, after a good week of digging, that the water table was higher than they thought. The hole they'd dug at the beach started filling with water after just three feet. They conveyed this information to the cabin group next switch day, and started to dig there instead. Which they should have done in any case. But the problem there was that after about a foot of digging, they hit bedrock. At every spot they tried.

Ike, or one of the others, continued to hack away at newly fallen trees with their only axe, and they continued to drag the huge chunks back to the cabin. When Ike wasn't using the axe, someone hacked away at the chunks, because as they were, they wouldn't fit into the woodstove. But it was near impossible. They thought about just burning the stuff in an outdoor fire, but that wouldn't warm the cabin. In any case, they'd need kindling, so they continued to forage for that, further and further every day.

So it was a day of celebration when Krush found an old hand saw at the dump. It had been underneath several feet of disgusting crap. Although it was rusty, and it fell apart when he picked it up, the blade was more or less intact. But they had no tape, no glue, no screws, no screwdriver— Ed went to their kindling pile, such as it was, and began fiddling with the saw. Two hours later, he presented the blade, newly fitted with a sort of wooden handle at each end.

"Hey!" John cried out. "Beautiful!"

He and Ed tried it out on a piece they carefully propped up off the ground. John immediately pulled the handle off his end of the blade.

"Shit, man, I'm sorry."

"Just jam it back on," Ed said, laughing. "And push the saw. Don't pull it."

"But you're supposed to do just the opposite!" John protested.

"No, you're supposed to just fill up your chainsaw with gas."

"You got that right," he grumbled, and they tried again.

If they were careful, and if they got into the right rhythm, it worked. Still it took two hours to saw off a chunk that would burn to ashes in just one hour.

"What's he doing?" LJ asked John one day, nodding at Anthony, who was sitting outside, alone, just staring into space.

"Listening."

"To what?" LJ looked around. "I don't hear anything."

"Don't know. Could be a Bach concert today," he smiled. Envious. Anthony had been doing what he was now doing every day since the CD player had gotten broken.

"He probably has whole symphonies in his head."

"Really?" LJ couldn't imagine having that much in his head.

16

A week later, on switch day, the beach group arrived at the cabin a little later than usual, having detoured here and there, looking for more dandelions—more everything, actually—and the still-elusive soapwort.

There was no one about. That's odd, they all thought. *Very* odd.

"Henry? Tapper? Anyone home?" John called out, already jogging toward the door. Ed went around back, and the rest started immediately to fan out toward the bush.

"In here!" John yelled, and as one, the others rushed inside.

Tapper was lying on the couch, pale, sweaty, and shivering.

"Water," he croaked. Then muttered something about being cold. So very cold.

"Get him some water!" John yelled. Tim grabbed the empty cup on the table and ran off to the well.

John felt Tapper's forehead. "He's burning up."

Ed in the meantime had gone to the bedrooms. "Juan and Henry are in here," he called out. "Henry's—Henry's unconscious. Juan's delirious," he said a few moments later.

"Ike," Anthony said, heading for the other bedroom. "Where's Ike?"

"Dead." Tapper groaned, his hands trembling as he took the cup Tim had given him.

"What happened?" John asked, taking the cup and helping him sit up a bit.

"Tim," Anthony said sharply. "Get out of here. You too

Biscuit, Krush, LJ."

"What'd I do—" Tim protested. They all looked confused.

"Could be contagious."

John looked up at Anthony. He was right. And he'd been practically breathing Tapper's exhalations. And Ed. Ed was in the small bedroom with the two of them.

"""You too, Anthony, go!" John said, then turned back to Tapper. "What happened?"

Tapper didn't respond. John grabbed the cup and went to the door.

Anthony was already there, with their one pail, freshly full. John nodded grimly, took the pail inside, poured another cup for Tapper, and gave it to him.

"Ed, we've got water out here!"

Ed came out of the small bedroom and filled a cup to take into Juan.

"Just suddenly—sick," Tapper managed to say.

"Was it something you ate maybe?" he asked. Hopefully.

"No. Nothing new."

"Anyone get bitten by something?"

"No."

Ed came out of the bedroom. "We gotta bring their fevers down," he said, looking around helplessly. "Too bad we're not at the beach, we could just throw them into the lake."

"Wet towels or something. We could—"

"Not a lot of extra towels around—" Ed took the pail into the bedroom and simply poured the rest of it onto Juan. It seemed to help. He took the empty pail back to the door, where Anthony was waiting. He took it wordlessly and went to refill it.

John searched the cabin for their only towel, soaked it in the refilled pail, and then covered Tapper's face with it.

Ed took off his own shirt, soaked it in the pail, and went back into the bedroom.

"How's Henry?" John called out.

"Breathing."

Anthony, Tim, Biscuit, Krush, and LJ were milling about near the door, anxiously waiting for an update, for instructions, for something that wouldn't make them feel so helpless.

A few moments later, John and Ed appeared. Anthony shepherded them all back a few yards.

"No offence," he said to John.

"None taken," John said. "Good idea."

"Henry's unconscious," Ed reported. "Juan's delirious."

"Tapper's coherent, but burning up. Any ideas?"

Anthony had been thinking hard. "Fever. Chills. Thirst. What else? Notice any rash?"

Ed shook his head, "No."

"Me neither," John said. "It wasn't something they ate. And no one got bit."

"Okay, so not food poisoning," Anthony reviewed. "Not rabies or distemper or anything like that. Too severe for any sort of flu."

"What else could it be?" Tim asked the obvious.

John punched the door frame in frustration. "We don't know! We don't know anything! We're just a bunch stupid—"

"Okay, let's keep it together," Anthony said, trying to keep them all calm. "We don't know. So we find out. LJ. When are you meeting your Mr. Morgan again?"

LJ thought a moment. "Today. It's supposed to be today!"

"Today?" Ed said. "I thought it was day *before* switch."

"It used to be. But last week he asked if he could change it."

"Well, how were you going to—"

"I hadn't figured it out yet. An' I forgot, okay?"

Ed threw up his hands in disgust and retreated back inside.

"It'll take four hours to get back to the beach, three if you hoof it," Anthony said, "then two hours from there. What time do you meet?"

"Mid-afternoon. Two."

John looked at his watch. "It's eleven now, he'll never make it."

"He can go the diagonal," Biscuit spoke up. "Might do it in three hours."

"The diagonal?"

"Yeah, instead of going back to the beach and then over, you take, like, the hypotenuse of the triangle." They stared at him. And he would have made some quip about having graduated from high school, but—

"But I don't know where—" LJ said helplessly. "I haven't—"

"I'll go with you," Biscuit said. "I know the way."

"Yeah? You can make it in three hours?" John asked.

"We can try. Anyone got a better idea?"

Silence.

So the two of them sprinted off.

17

Fifteen minutes later, they were running.

An hour after that, jogging.

Open country, then bush, then open country again.

They kept going. As fast as they could. Given.

Finally they arrived, almost walking, at a road. It must have been a logging road at some point. Biscuit was completely exhausted.

"It's one-thirty," he panted, bent over, looking at his watch. "And it's at least another five miles. We're never going to make it."

"Five miles just straight on this road?" LJ asked, panting as well. "And then I'm at the window?" Now that he thought of it, he had noticed a road at the window that went off in another direction, but he'd never bothered to find out where it went.

"Yeah—well, not straight, but—"

"I can do it."

Biscuit looked up at him in disbelief. "That's six minutes a mile!"

"I know," he said, a little uncertainly.

"After what we just did?"

"I can do it," he said again, this time with resolve.

"All right," Biscuit said. "Go! I'll catch up. Do it, man! Just do it!" he grinned, cheering him on.

LJ took off at a near sprint.

About half an hour later—he didn't know exactly, because he didn't have a watch, and didn't think to ask for

Biscuit's—not that he would have parted with his precious Daffy Duck—LJ arrived and approached the window, completely winded, hoping he wasn't too late.

"Mr. Morgan!" he called out feebly, then bent over and gulped oxygen.

There was no answer.

"Mr. Morgan—you there?" he straightened up and called out more loudly.

Still no answer.

"Mr. Morgan!" He stumbled a little to his left and called out, then did the same to the right, trying to find the exact spot. "Mr. Morgan!"

"LJ?"

He took a few steps in the direction of his voice. "They're all sick—Tapper—Henry—Juan," he said, still panting, "and we need to know—what to do—"

"Slow down," Mr. Morgan said. He understood immediately that something was wrong. "Catch your breath. You ran all the way here?"

"Didn't want to miss you," LJ's heart rate was starting to return to normal, and his breathing was becoming a little less laboured. "They're all sick," he repeated. "We need to bring down their fever. We don't know what it is."

"Could be just the flu or something," Mr. Morgan suggested.

"Ike's dead."

"Oh— I'm— I'm so sorry." Seriously wrong. "Could it have been food poisoning?"

"They said they didn't eat anything new. And it's not rabies or anything, no one's been bit. They're hot, but cold, and thirsty," LJ tried to think of everything that could be relevant. "Henry's in a coma or something, and Juan's delirious. Happened fast, I think."

"Okay, okay," Mr. Morgan was thinking, as quickly as he could, "So yes, if you can bring down the fever …"

"Do you know how to bring down a fever?"

"Well, our daughter had a fever once. We gave her Tylenol, I believe."

"We ain't got no Tylenol!" LJ screamed in frustration. He started pacing, back and forth, before his legs cramped.

"No, of course not. Sorry. But yes," he understood now, "there must be some plant that does the same thing." He tried to remember—he didn't think there had been anything about medicinal uses in the book he'd had. Perhaps another book—

"Can you find out for us?" LJ asked. "I can't pay now, but I will. I promise. Somehow."

"Yes, I'm sure you will," he didn't care about that. Where was the nearest library? He was already heading for his car. "I'll be back as soon as I can," he turned and shouted.

"Okay. Please—"

Mr. Morgan drove off as quickly as he dared on the unpaved road, mentally cursing himself—his daughter had *told* him he should've gotten the 'smartcar' option and if he'd listened to her, he could've found out right then and there what LJ and his friends needed to know.

There were several towns along the highway that led to the road that led to the window, but he couldn't remember now just how far away the nearest one was. And he certainly didn't know if it had a library.

The car's automated system suddenly interrupted his thoughts. "The gas tank is almost empty. Please fill up. The gas tank is almost empty. Please fill—"

He reached out with irritation and turned off the audio. Then slapped his hand on the steering wheel, glanced at the gas gauge, and tried to remember where the nearest gas station was.

As soon as Mr. Morgan left, LJ stopped pacing and sank to his knees. He'd done it! He'd gotten here in time and delivered their SOS. He wasn't at all sure it would be enough, but …

A few minutes later, he got back up and began stretching. It had suddenly dawned on him that he was going to have to run all the way back. Before it got dark.

He wished he'd thought to bring a bottle of water.

He wondered where the nearest stream was.

Biscuit might know.

But Biscuit hadn't arrived yet.

In fact, he wasn't even in sight yet.

Mr. Morgan pulled into a gas station on an empty stretch of the highway. He got out, quickly filled the tank, then went inside to pay.

"Say, do you happen to know where the nearest library is?" he asked the attendant.

"No, sorry."

A few miles later, he passed another gas station, a restaurant, and a couple of abandoned buildings. Rather than waste time looking for someone who might or might not know where the nearest library was, he drove on.

He slowed at the "Treville, Pop. 3,000" sign, and carefully looked at the few buildings that lined the main street. Which was actually still the highway. What would a library in such a small town look like? He had no idea. When he saw a post office, he pulled over to go in and ask. As he hurried up the steps, he saw a small sign pointing to a side entrance: *Treville Public Library*. Perfect.

LJ looked anxiously down the road again, such as it was, but he still didn't see Biscuit. Even if he was walking the whole way, shouldn't he be seeing him by now? Well, no, maybe he was around the curve. Should he go look for him? He had no idea how long Mr. Morgan would be. And he wouldn't see or hear his car, to know to turn back. He didn't think he'd show up, then leave if he wasn't there, but every minute counted, and if he wasn't right there—

The library was one room in the basement of the post office. Three walls were full of books; the fourth was full of magazines. A children's story time corner was at one end of the room; a computer station was at the other. Mr. Morgan walked up to the desk in the middle of the room.

"Hello, may I help you?" the middle-aged woman smiled.

"Yes, I hope so. I'm looking for some information. I'm trying to find out what plants, what wild plants, will bring down a fever."

"Oh, I'm sure we have some field guides or survival-in-the-wild books that will have that information for you," she said. "They would be in the Geography section," she nodded toward one of the walls.

"I'm afraid I'm in a bit of a hurry—" Mr. Morgan looked helplessly at the shelves she had indicated.

"Oh, then perhaps a computer search would be best. Joshua—"

The young man who was at the computer station turned.

"Could you please help this gentleman do a quick computer search?"

"Sure. What are you looking for?"

"Wild plants that will bring down a fever." Mr. Morgan went to stand at the young man's shoulder.

"Okay …" Joshua entered the keywords into the search engine. "Looks like there's almost fifty—"

"Can we narrow it down a bit somehow?"

"Sure, are you interested in any particular area?"

"Yes, this one. Well, within—fifty miles?" He had no idea how far LJ and his group travelled from their home base. Wherever that was.

"Okay ..." Joshua did a bit of keyboarding. "That leaves us with ten. Some die off by early summer—"

"You can eliminate those."

"Okay ... so we have seven left. Oh, that one's pretty—" he pointed to the screen, to a spiny, purple flower.

"I know that one," Mr. Morgan said, surprised. "Bergamot. Mrs. Emerson—a friend of mine has that in her garden, I think."

Joshua read the text beside the image. "You're right. It says it's wild bergamot. Rather common. Now this one," he pointed to another picture, "it says this one's rare."

"Could we eliminate those as well? If we just stick with the ones that are easy to find, in this area, this time of year, how many are there?"

"That brings us down to four. The wild bergamot, willow, wild licorice, and lemon verbena."

"Four's good. That's—and all of those grow this far north? This time of year?" He was surprised.

"Says so," Joshua double-checked. "Maybe with the climate change... Certain plants have the ability to migrate ..."

"Right. I guess they would ..."

"Would you like me to print this out?"

"Yes, please."

"Pictures, descriptions—do you want the 'What to do with it' part too?"

"Yes, please."

"And what about the 'How it works' part?"

"No, that you don't need to print."

"Okay ..." He moved the mouse and clicked. "Done.

And … here you go," he said, taking four sheets of paper from the printer under the desk and handing them to Mr. Morgan. "You can pay at the other desk—twenty-five cents per page."

"Okay. Thank you very much."

Mr. Morgan hurried back to the center desk, paid the dollar, and left. It was that easy. Thanks to a long line, a very long line, of people—botanists, physicians, photographers, writers, publishers, website designers, computer technicians, satellite dish engineers, internet service providers, paper manufacturers, ink producers …

LJ trotted about half a mile along the road to the curve, but there was still no sign of Biscuit. He continued to be torn between going further to find Biscuit and turning back to be at the window when Mr. Morgan returned. He trotted back to the window. On the one hand, Biscuit, the slacker, was probably just taking his sweet time. On the other hand, he remembered Krush's "And we never go anywhere alone."

Mr. Morgan pulled off the road, but didn't bother to park neatly like he usually did. He fumbled with his seat belt, then strode quickly toward the window, the four sheets of paper in his hand.

"LJ? Are you still there?"

"Mr. Morgan?"

LJ straightened from stretching his hamstrings. "Did you find something?"

"I think so. There are a few possibilities. I've got pictures, but of course you can't see them. First, there's wild bergamot—do you know what that looks like?"

"No."

"It has purple flowers. Looks a bit like a sea anemone—you know what that is?"

"Yeah, like an octopus sort of." How the hell did he know that? He had no idea.

"That's it. It grows to about three feet. You grind the plant to a powder and rub it over the body," Mr. Morgan read from the sheet.

"Okay," LJ said, then asked, "What else?"

"Willow bark. You know what a willow tree looks like?"

"Yes." He was surprising himself.

"Good, okay, it's the bark you want. You make a tea."

"Okay, anything else?"

"Yes, two more. Wild licorice. I guess that'll smell like licorice. It looks—well it's about four feet high, it says, has dark green leaves, and yellow and white pea-like flowers. Grows in ditches and near slow streams."

LJ started to panic. He was already getting the three feet tall and the four feet tall mixed up, and the purple, and yellow, and white—

"I'm not going to be able to remember all this!" he moaned in despair. "I can't—"

"Yes, you can," Mr. Morgan assured him, calmed him. "Let's go back. What was the first one."

"I don't remember!"

"Looks like an—"

"An octopus! A purple octopus!"

"Good. How tall?"

"Four feet?"

"Close enough probably. Three feet. And what do you do with it?"

"Make tea—no, you rub the flowers—"

"You grind the plant and rub the powder over the body. Say it all."

"Purple octopus, three feet tall, grind the plant and rub it—no, rub the powder over the body. Okay. I think I've got it."

"And the second one?"

"That was the willow tree—tea from the bark."

"Good. The third one was wild licorice." Mr. Morgan thought for a few seconds. "Maybe this'll help. Picture a licorice stick like you might've had as a kid, yeah? Okay, now put dark green leaves on the licorice stick, got it? In your mind? Now add small yellow and white flowers to the licorice stick. Make the thing four feet tall and put it in a ditch. A four-foot-tall licorice stick with dark green leaves and little white and yellow flowers. Got it?"

"Yeah, it looks stupid—"

"Well that's not actually what you'll be looking for, you understand. It's just to help you remember what kind of leaves and flowers wild licorice has."

"Okay, what do we do with it if I find it?"

"That one you can make a tea from the roots or you can chew the roots. I guess that'd be quicker, maybe stronger. Have your sick people chew the roots while you're waiting for the water to boil.

"Okay, one more. Lemon verbena. Smells like lemon, again dark green leaves, again small flowers, but this time mauve and white. And again, make a tea."

"Make a tea. Okay." LJ started to head off down the path.

"Wait!" Mr. Morgan cried out when he realized LJ had left. "Are you sure you've got it all? Come back and say it to me."

"There's no time!" LJ protested.

"But if you don't get it right, it won't matter!"

He had a point. LJ returned, struggling to be patient, struggling to concentrate.

"Say it," Mr. Morgan prompted.

"Purple octopus, three feet tall, tea. Willow bark, grind it and put the powder—"

"No," Mr. Morgan cut in, "the purple octopus gets

ground to a powder. Imagine grinding a purple octopus—"
An unpleasant image, but—

"Purple octopus, three feet tall, grind it to a powder and put it on the body."

"Good. Next."

"Willow bark tea."

"Good. Next."

LJ thought. He couldn't remember.

"Smells like…"

"Licorice. Four feet tall, dark green leaves and yellow and white flowers and—" He couldn't remember what to do with it.

"The roots get chewed—like real licorice, yeah? Or made into a tea. And the last one?"

"The last one was—I can't remember!" he cried out, hitting his head with his fist. They should've sent someone else! Where was Biscuit? He could help remember!

"You can do this, LJ. Just think a minute. It's another one you can smell—"

"Lemon! Lemon something. Dark green leaves again, small flowers again, but mauve and white. Tea."

"Okay, once more. All of it."

LJ recited the information one more time.

"Okay, I think you've got it," Mr. Morgan said. "Keep saying it, and look for the stuff as you go. Good luck!"

As LJ ran down the road, managing to sprint all the way to the curve and then some, he started muttering to himself, all the bits of information about the four plants. He wished he could have put it into a song or a rhyme like Anthony had done. But imagining himself grinding a purple octopus helped, as did the licorice stick with the green leaves and yellow flowers. He looked for the plants as he ran, glancing from one side of the road to the other—

No. Oh, no.

He scrambled down into the ditch.

Biscuit. He'd been beaten pretty badly. His shoes and most of his clothes were gone, and his Daffy Duck watch was smashed.

He knelt beside him, helplessly, then put his hand on his shoulder and shook him just a little. "Biscuit! Say something, man!" But LJ knew he was dead. He'd known it as soon as he'd seen him.

"No, no, no ..." He pulled Biscuit onto his lap, and started rocking back and forth. Started crying. It was all just too much.

After a moment, he looked around desperately. He didn't have time to bury him, and he didn't have a shovel in any case, and there weren't enough rocks around to cover him up. He picked him up, set him carefully over his shoulder, then climbed back out of the ditch. But it was hopeless. He couldn't carry him all the way back, and even if he could, it would slow him down terribly. But he couldn't just leave him there.

Suddenly he heard the whooping war cries in the distance. Shit! They were coming back. He tenderly but quickly set Biscuit back down, back into the ditch, a little hidden at least. He gave him one last look, took off his watch, put it in deep into his pocket—then ran like hell.

Half an hour later, he realized he had outrun the beaters. He was exhausted, but still moving.

He started reciting the information again, and started looking again for purple octopus flowers, willow trees, wild licorice plants, and lemon somethings.

An hour later, with bunches of flowers and plants

sticking out of his pockets, and chunks of bark in his hands, he suddenly realized he didn't know where he was. He stopped, and began to lose it. Again. Then he saw a bent tree in the distance. It was familiar. Biscuit had made a joke about it on the way. LJ was about a mile on the wrong side of it. He began to run again, toward the tree.

Three hours after that, just as it was starting to get dark, he staggered toward the cabin. His pockets were full. He had taken off his shirt and tied it into a bag which he carried in his right hand. It was bulging. He had a bunch of uprooted plants in his other hand. All of it more or less fit the descriptions given by Mr. Morgan.

Krush, Tim, and Anthony were out front, anxiously waiting for him, looking for him. When they spotted him, they ran out to meet him, all talking at once.

"LJ—"

"Did you make it in time?"

"You've got something?"

LJ put his hand up to quiet them, collected himself, then spoke very clearly and pointedly to each one in turn.

"Purple octopus," he said to Anthony, "four feet tall, grind the plant to a powder, rub it on."

Anthony nodded, then stepped aside.

"Willow bark tea," LJ said to Krush.

Krush nodded.

"Licorice," he said to Tim. "Three feet tall, dark green leaves, mauve and white flowers. Chew the roots or make tea."

"Got it," Tim said after a moment, then stepped away, mumbling it to himself.

"Lemon something," LJ called out to John, standing in the doorway. "Dark green leaves, yellow and white tiny flowers. Tea." He nodded.

LJ emptied his hands then, and his shirt bag, and his pockets. Krush rushed to help him when he fumbled. Once everything was laid out on the ground, Anthony began to sort it.

"Where's Biscuit?" Tim asked quietly then, having looked in the distance several times, expecting him—

LJ just looked at him helplessly.

"No," Anthony looked up. "No—" he repeated, shaking his head as if that could—

"I went on ahead once we got to the road. He told me to. We had only half an hour left, and it was five miles—"

"They beat him bad?" Krush asked.

LJ nodded.

"FUCK this place!!" he bellowed for all of them, heaving LJ's empty shirt bag at—nothing.

18

Five minutes later, Tapper was chewing on what was, hopefully, wild licorice.

John was boiling water on the woodstove. He'd set out two cups, and put some willow bark in one and some of the lemon something in the other.

Ed had made a powder out of what was, he hoped, the right kind of purple octopus. He looked at it dubiously, then took it into the bedroom. Henry was still unconscious, but he rubbed the stuff onto his chest anyway. He would've liked to have had his consent, since it could, of course, just make things worse, but he reasoned that Henry would've said yes. They didn't really have any choice but to experiment on each other this way.

Once the tea was made, John gave the first cup to Tapper and took the other into the bedroom where he helped Juan, barely conscious, drink from it.

Next day, John and Ed carried Henry's body out of the cabin and lay it beside Ike's, some distance away.

Anthony, Krush, and Tim searched for more plants that fit the descriptions LJ had given them, bringing back scraps for the woodstove, if nothing else.

LJ couldn't move. He felt like he'd torn every single muscle in his body and then some, running what must have been almost two marathons in one day. So he just sat outside and started building another rabbit trap.

Ed became sick that evening and lay on the bed Henry had occupied.

Day three, John and Anthony carried out Juan's body

and put it down beside the bodies of Henry and Ike.

Tapper sat up on the couch, apparently recovering.

Anthony, Krush, and Tim searched for more wild licorice.

LJ stripped as much bark as he could from the nearby willow tree, and John made more tea at the woodstove.

Day four, John became sick and took Juan's place in the bedroom. LJ made more willow tea and gave it to John, along with the licorice.

Day five, Anthony and Tim carried out Ed's body.

On day six, things seemed to hold steady—

Then on day seven—on day seven, Anthony came out of the cabin, carrying Tim's body. He walked to where the other bodies lay. The other men—Krush, LJ, Tapper, and John—formed a short line behind him.

Still holding Tim, for he couldn't let him go, not yet, not ever, Anthony sang. An anguished lament, so pure, so—

When the last note ended, when Anthony had exhaled his last bit of breath, he tenderly set Tim beside the others. LJ stepped forward then and put Biscuit's shattered watch into one of Tim's hands.

19

A month later, LJ walked to the window. He hadn't even said thank you yet.

"Mr. Morgan?" he called out, not very loudly, and not really expecting an answer. It had been a while.

"He ain't here." It was a younger voice. A sullen voice. "You LJ?" It challenged.

"Yeah," LJ replied. "Who are you?"

And then, since it suddenly occurred to him—"Is Mr. Morgan all right?"

"The trashman—"

"His name is Mr. Morgan," LJ said. Insisted.

"Whatever. He sent me here."

"Why?" LJ was confused.

"He said somethin' about a payment you had to make. Said you had somethin' to say to me."

LJ was confused. He *had* promised to pay for the information, but—

"You still there?"

"Yeah, I—" Then he understood. And smiled. Sort of.

"So," the young man on the other side spat onto the ground, to show his contempt for the world, for everything and everyone in it, "you got somethin' to say to me or not?"

About the Author

Peg Tittle has published one previous novella, *What Happened to Tom* (Inanna, 2016); two more works of fiction are forthcoming from Inanna, *It Wasn't Enough* (2020) and *Impact* (2021). She is also the author of *Sexist Shit that Pisses Me Off* (2018), *What If...: Collected Thought Experiments in Philosophy* (2004), and *Critical Thinking: An Appeal to Reason* (2011), and the editor of *Should Parents be Licensed?: Debating the Issues* (2004). Her articles and essays have been published in a number of North American magazines and journals, and she has been a columnist for the Institute for Ethics and Emerging Technologies, *The Philosophers' Magazine*, and *Philosophy Now*.

Writing comedic fiction as Jass Richards, she has published *This Will Not Look Good on My Resume* (2010), *The Road Trip Dialogues* (2011), *The Blasphemy Tour* (2012), *License to Do That* (2014), *Dogs Just Wanna Have Fun* (2014), and *TurboJetslams: Proof #29 of the Non-Existence of God* (2016). *A Philosopher, a Psychologist, and an Extraterrestrial Walk into a Chocolate Bar* is forthcoming (2018) from Lacuna. Her work has appeared in *The Cynic Online Magazine*, *Contemporary Monologues for Young Women* (vol. 3), and *222 More Comedy Monologues*, as well as on Erma Bombeck's humor website, and her one-woman play, *Supply Teacher from Hell*, received its premiere performance by Ghost Monkey Productions in Winnipeg.

pegtittle.com
jassrichards.com

Lightning Source UK Ltd.
Milton Keynes UK
UKHW041509210219
337759UK00001B/32/P

9 781772 441611